——— **Jean Wills** ———

AMY AT THE
BAKERY

The crowd stopped. Faces looked down on her. Voices spoke.

'Isn't that Amy at the Bakery?'

'Lift the little lass up. She'll never see anything from down there.'

So up she went, over the heads. Opposite was a big new shop. THE SUNNY STORES, with enormous glass windows and its own car park. Just stepping out of one of the cars was . . . Andy Tearovski. Amy recognised him from Brian's pictures.

Jean Wills

AMY AT THE BAKERY

Illustrated by Mary Rees

Hippo Books
Scholastic Publications Limited
London

Scholastic Publications Ltd.,
10 Earlham Street, London WC2H 9RX, UK

Scholastic Inc.,
730 Broadway, New York, NY 10003, USA

Scholastic Canada Ltd.,
123 Newkirk Road, Richmond Hill,
Ontario L4C 3G5, Canada

Ashton Scholastic Pty Ltd.,
P O Box 579, Gosford, New South Wales,
Australia

Ashton Scholastic Ltd.,
Private Bag 1, Penrose, Auckland,
New Zealand

First published by Andersen Press Ltd., 1990
This edition published by Scholastic Publications Ltd., 1991

Text copyright © Jean Wills, 1990
Illustration copyright © Andersen Press Ltd, 1990

ISBN 0 590 76419 5

All rights reserved

Typeset by AKM Associates (UK) Ltd, Southall, London

Contents

To Adam, Shani and Robert

WELCOME TO STEEPLE FOLEY says the notice on the main road. Above is a picture of a tall church steeple and a wriggling river.

Carry straight on.

A stretch of houses, roads off, a Junior school, and you come to the bottom of the High Street. First on the right is Jersey Joe's, the second-hand shop. Go on up, past the other shops almost to the very top. There it is, on the right-hand side, the smallest shop of all. EAST'S BAKERY.

The window is piled with doughnuts, buns, fancies, flans. Cherry cake, marble cake, coffee cake, sultana cake . . . .

Step inside, and if you're tall, mind your head. If it's crowded, breathe in. More than four customers at once is a squash.

Behind the counter on the right stands Mrs East, in a clean apron, and Baby Roy in his pram. In the left-hand corner a wedding cake with six tiers.

When Mrs East's not looking peep through the curtain at the back made of plastic strips. You'll see a passage leading to the kitchen, and you might even catch sight of Mr East at his ovens.

And, if they're not at school, Amy who is seven, and her brother Brian, eight and a half. You're almost sure to see their dog, Fruity. He spends most of his time behind the curtain, waiting for something to happen . . . .

1
Amy Goes Sorting

One wild March afternoon, when the wind rattled the shop door and set the paper bags rustling, Mrs East called, 'Fred? I've something to tell you. *Fred*!'

Mr East, all floury from baking, bowled through the curtain.

'Yes, my dear?'

Mrs East nodded at Amy, who'd just returned from school. 'It's Amy.'

'I know that, my love.'

'This is no joke, Fred. A customer has *complained*.'

Mr East raised his floury eyebrows. 'About our Amy?'

His wife nodded. 'After all I've taught her.'

The pram behind the counter shook. Baby Roy had woken up. 'I'll tell your father, Amy.' Mrs East nodded at the baby. 'You carry him upstairs.'

'What, carry Dad?'

'Do you see, Fred East?' his wife said. 'It's you sets your children a bad example.'

Lifting Baby Roy out of the pram Amy hurried through the curtain. She went past the coats and up the stairs. Fruity followed. *Swish, thump*, went his tail, all the way to the top.

Baby Roy was six months old, but growing heavier every day. Amy was glad to put him down.

She fetched their favourite book. Although it was spotted with stains and splodges it was very grand. *Cakes and Pastries of the World.*

They sat together on the sofa. Baby Roy on Amy's lap, and the book propped against the back.

'And now . . .' Amy reached forward '. . . as the earwig said as he fell over the cliff . . .' Baby Roy gurgled, tried to clap his hands but missed. '. . . 'ere we *GO*!'

She turned to the page with the waffles, like

little golden gates, and picked out two. They gobbled away. Baby Roy on his bald gums. Amy smacking her lips.

When Mrs East came up Baby Roy decided it was real food he wanted.

While he was having his bottle Brian arrived with his friend Red. Baby Roy stopped sucking and all the air came out of the bottle, fizzzzz . . . The boys began to giggle.

'I can't do with you two fooling about,' Mrs East told them.

When they went into the front bedroom Amy followed. Red and Brian climbed the ladder to Brian's top bunk. They knelt with their faces to the wall which was covered in pictures of racing cars and famous drivers.

'We'll soon have enough,' Red said.

'Enough what?' Amy asked.

They wouldn't tell her. *All right*, Amy thought. *She* wouldn't tell *them* about the complaining customer. Though she longed to tell somebody . . . .

Crawling into her bottom bunk she looked at *her* picture. She only had one. St. Paul's Cathedral, from last year's calendar. Amy hadn't been to London yet, but one day she would.

She got up and opened the window.

CRASH!

The March wind almost dragged her out. A bus pulled up at the stop outside. The passengers on top watched her trying to shut the window.

Brian and Red pushed her aside.

'If that glass had broken!' Brian fastened the latch.

'You'd have killed those people down below,' Red said cheerfully. 'Cut their heads clean off, snick-snack.'

Mrs East came running in with the baby. Amy was in trouble again. Then Mr East called from the shop.

'The four o'clock rush!' The bakery was always busy after the mothers had collected their children from school and plodded up the hill. Mrs East handed Baby Roy back to Amy. 'Bring him down and put on his coat. Then you can take him to the park.' Fruity began to get excited. 'And I don't want no more trouble.'

Brian and Red turned round from the wall. 'What trouble?'

So then Amy had to tell about the complaining customer.

'She said I let Fruity run wild in the park and chase the ducks. And I didn't. He only barked. And . . . .'

'*And*?' said Brian.

'She said I was rude.'

'What did you say to her?'

'Nothing special. It's just sometimes I get cross because you go off and leave me to look after everything by myself.'

'So now it's our fault,' Red said.

Amy carried Baby Roy downstairs and took down his coat. She zipped him inside and fastened his hood. Then she put on her own.

Brian fastened Fruity's lead while Red hauled out the pram from behind the counter. The customer nearest the door had to go outside to make way for the children. Of course it would have to be the complaining customer back again.

She pointed to the notice on the door. SORRY, NO DOGS.

'Fruity's *our* dog,' Brian said. 'And he's not allowed in the shop, nor the kitchen neither.'

'But he *was* in the shop.'

'We got to get him *out*,' said Brian.

The complaining customer opened her mouth to go on complaining, but an extra big gust of wind blew up the High Street. It went inside the hood of the pram, and they set off in a great hurry.

Fruity tugging at his lead, they shot past the hairdresser's, the jeweller's, the Midland Bank, and round the corner by the church.

It was downhill all the way to the park, but Red and Brian stopped by the alley which ran along behind the shops. Brian shared out the broken biscuits which he'd taken from the bin behind the bakery counter.

Over the top of the pramhood Amy could see the Foley River which ran through the park. Ducks rode roller coaster waves.

Brian held out Fruity's lead, but Amy shook her head.

'Listen,' Brian said. 'I got to go with Red . . . .'

'It's not fair!'

'Listen. It's only for one more time.'

14

'No.'

'All right,' Red said. 'We'll take her with us.'

'Pram and dog and all? What will *she* say?'

'We'll soon find out.'

Red jerked Fruity into the alley. Brian took over the pram. Amy was left to follow behind.

'Quiet passing *yours*,' Red warned.

They crept along behind the fences, the pram bumping, until Red stopped. He climbed up and over the top, opened his gate from the other side, and they all trooped in.

The back yard of Pepper's, the greengrocer's, was very different from the front. On show in the High Street was the pick of the fruit and vegetables. Oranges, lemons, apples, pears. Mangoes, grapefruit, bunches of bananas. Shiny onions, purple cabbage, cauliflower as white as foam, But here . . .

Amy was about to hold her nose when she saw Red's great-gran watching her from inside her sentry-box.

'What's this lot?' The old lady, wrinkled as a prune, pointed at Amy. 'Who's she?'

'Amy at the Bakery,' Red said. 'And her and Brian's baby brother.'

Great-Gran pointed to the pram. 'Bring it here.'

As she stuck her head inside, Baby Roy began to laugh. He thought Great-Gran's wrinkled prune face the funniest thing he'd ever seen.

'*Sludge*!' said Great-Gran admiringly. 'What a pair of gums!'

Then a terrible thing happened. Great-Gran Pepper put her hand in her mouth and . . . took her teeth right out! She put them down on some watercress. There they sat like waterlilies.

'Stop showing off,' Red told her. 'Me and Brian are here to sort.'

Great-Gran put her teeth back in. 'Carrots,' she said, then pointed to Amy. 'What about her?'

Amy didn't know.

Great-Gran leaned forward. 'Like to buy pretty things, don't you?' She tossed a mouldy potato into the rubbish bin. 'I liked pretty things once. Then I went and married a greengrocer. Don't ever do that, dearie.'

Amy shook her head.

'Well, let's see how you are sortin' then.'

Great-Gran nodded at the potato sack. 'Damp's got in. Sort the bad 'uns and chuck 'em out. See you don't miss any, mind.'

Amy enjoyed herself sorting. In fact she forgot about everything else, until Fruity barked.

Poor Fruity. He'd never even set paw in the park. Instead he'd been made to sit quiet on a pile of smelly old cabbage leaves. But now, moving across the bottom fence like a tightrope walker came . . . a black cat!'

'That's lucky, that is,' Great-Gran said.

'Not for us,' said Amy. 'Fruity, *stay*!' But already it was too late. Fruity had taken a scrambling leap, right over the top of the fence. He vanished barking up the alley.

Amy glanced at Baby Roy. 'Oh *no!*'

Baby Roy was sucking an orange. And he was covered! Face, hands, coat, everything. Sticky as a lily's stamen.

As Amy snatched the orange away Baby Roy screamed.

'Cruel,' said the old lady.

'But he's only a baby, six months old. He hasn't even got any teeth!'

17

'*Sludge*! Don't need teeth to suck an orange. And pips don't hurt. When Red was in his pram he was always swallowing 'em.'

'No I wasn't,' Red said.

'How do you know?' Brian asked. Then he saw Amy and his mouth dropped open. 'Look at you!'

Amy looked at herself. The potatoes were covered with sooty soil, and so was she!

'Why couldn't *I* have done carrots?' she asked angrily.

'Carrots is for experts,' Red said. 'Anyhow, we've finished.'

Great-Gran beckoned from her sentry-box. 'Bring them here and let me see. If you've missed any bad 'uns customers'll find 'em.' She poked about the carrots. Then she nodded, paid Red and Brian, and passed a coin into Amy's hand. 'Hold on tight to that, dearie. Money don't grow on trees.'

They went back along the alley.

'Mum'll have a fit,' Amy whispered. 'I'll be in worse trouble than ever.'

'If we could get in the back way she needn't see us.' Brian stood on Red's shoulders and climbed over the bakery fence. After he'd let them in they pushed the pram across the yard and into the kitchen.

It was lovely and warm after the draughty greengrocer's yard and windy alley. There was hot madeira cake fresh out of the oven. Baby Roy began to coo.

'Shush,' said Amy. Brian ran upstairs for the dummy.

'Fruity's back,' he whispered when he returned. 'He must have slipped in the shop door without anybody noticing.'

Amy gave Baby Roy the dummy and cleaned him up. Then she stood on a chair by the big sink and started on herself. She'd almost finished when . . . .

Out from the store cupboard stepped Mr East, holding a bag of flour and a big tin of jam.

'Little heart-shaped shortbreads,' said Mr East, 'with a raspberry jam filling.'

Amy and Brian looked at each other. It was all right! Their father wouldn't have noticed if they'd turned sky blue pink. He was *inventing*!

'Anybody would think,' said Mrs East at tea-time, 'that *somebody* had been digging up a potato field.' Amy had missed her nails!

Brian had the giggles. Until his mother looked *him* over. 'Why are your hands orange?'

He mumbled something about paint at school, and was sent to wash it off.

Then Mrs East swore she could smell cabbage. 'It's coming from under the table. Has that dog been rolling in something?'

Next she found Baby Roy's dummy. 'Why is this all sticky?'

But Mr East was reaching down *Cakes and Pastries of the World.* 'Would you help me find a name, my dear?'

It wasn't every day of the year that new cakes were invented. Mrs East thought and thought, and said at last, 'How about . . . *Little Darlings*?'

Brian said over his dead body.

Then Amy said, 'Why not just plain *jammy hearts*?' And nobody could find anything wrong with that.

Later on, lying in her bottom bunk, Amy asked Brian what he and Red were doing with their sorting money.

'Saving.'

'What for?'

'Something.'

Baby Roy sighed in his sleep in his cot, and Brian wouldn't say any more.

After school the next day Amy went and looked in Jersey Joe's second-hand shop for something pretty. But nothing really took her fancy, so she stopped at Pepper's instead for a large shiny apple.

The complaining customer was waiting in the bakery. When it was her turn she complained that the crust on yesterday's bread had been burnt, and the buns stale. Mrs East looked amazed. Then the complaining customer told her that Fruity had rushed from the alley in Church Way, knocked her off her feet, and chased a cat up a tree in the churchyard.

'Oh no,' said Mrs East decidedly. 'Fruity was in the park yesterday. *That* I do know. Ask Amy.'

But Amy had disappeared through the curtain with Baby Roy.

2
Amy and the Hot Cross Buns

'Yummy!'

Amy rolled out of her bunk. She went and opened the door a crack and took a big sniff. Then she gave a big smile.

'Brian, wake up.'

Her brother turned over in the top bunk and hit his head on the wall.

'Ow!'

''It's Hot Cross buns,' Amy said.

Brian felt his head and moaned. 'I was doing a hundred and sixty an hour in a Ferrari! Just coming up to overtake Andy Tearovski, when . . . CRASH! It's you saying Hot Cross buns.'

'Well, so it is.'

Brian turned his face to the wall. To the racing cars and famous drivers.

Amy went and looked in the cot. Baby Roy was still asleep, one hand raised in a tiny fist.

There was no school today because it was Saturday, *and* the holidays had started. They'd started at half past three yesterday, but it was only now they felt real. Easter holidays. And Hot Cross buns for starters.

Above the jeweller's next to the Midland Bank was a big clock. It had three faces which stuck out over the road. By pressing her nose on the window Amy could see the time. Nearly half past six.

Soon the first bus stopped outside. Baby Roy woke up. Fruity came nosing in at the door. The day had really started now.

At eight o'clock Fruity sat under the table hedged in by chairlegs and feet. Amy's and Brian's. Mr East's, all floury from the early baking. Mrs East's next to Baby Roy's dangling from his high chair.

'Red gets his own breakfast,' Brian grumbled. 'Just when he feels like it.'

'I can't help what those Peppers get up to.'

Mrs East smoothed her apron. 'The rule here is breakfast at eight o'clock sharp.'

Brian rested his feet on Fruity's comfortable back. 'I bet Andy Tearovski doesn't have rules.'

Mr East raised his floury eyebrows. 'Oh, don't you?'

Before Brian could argue Mrs East said, 'And instead of doing your usual disappearing act you can help your father with the trays.'

Brian made a face but he didn't really mind. Carrying trays through to the shop meant filling his pockets with treats for later. Even Andy Tearovski couldn't do that.

When Brian had followed his father downstairs Mrs East nodded at Amy. 'I'm behind an' all. You finish up here, while I go down and do the shop.'

'Oh Mum.' Amy had been looking forward to arranging thc sticky Hot Cross buns in the window, and sucking her fingers afterwards.

'You can help if you're quick.'

Amy cleared the table. Piling the dishes in the sink she turned on the hot water and squirted in washing-up liquid. *A good soak first and the job's half-done* was Mrs East's rule for washing-up.

'Come and play,' Baby Roy said in baby language.

'Can't,' said Amy. 'And hurry, do. I'll miss the Hot Cross buns else.' As Baby Roy opened his mouth she slid a spoonful of cereal inside. 'And don't you dare to spit it out!'

After he'd drunk his fruit juice she wiped his face and changed his nappy.

'Hot Cross bums,' she sang as Baby Roy kicked his chubby little legs in the air, 'One a penny, two a penny. Hot Cross bums.'

Amy carried him downstairs and Fruity followed. *Swish, thump*! As far as the curtain.

While Amy was strapping Baby Roy into his pram Brian slid a tray of doughnuts on the counter. He put out his tongue and licked off some sugar.

Amy giggled and Mrs East looked over. 'Finished?' she asked.

'Yes, Mum,' Amy said.

'Washed your hands?'

Oh no! She'd forgotten *them*! Pushing through the curtain again she jumped over

Fruity and flew upstairs. When she came down she was just in time to put the last Hot Cross bun on top of the pile.

'Now stack these loaves behind the counter,' Mrs East went on. 'And hurry, do. We haven't all day.'

The church clock began to strike. As the last chime died away Mrs East unbolted the door, and turned the notice from CLOSED to OPEN.

Amy and Brian took Baby Roy and Fruity to the park. When they came back the top Hot Cross bun was still on the pile in the window.

One of Mrs East's rules was . . . *Never be pushy with customers, let them make up their own minds.* Unlike Brian and Amy, who had to do as they were told. So Amy was surprised to hear her mother say, 'No Hot Cross buns today?'

'Just my weekend usual,' said the customer.

Mrs East wrapped up two loaves. 'Nobody wants our Hot Cross buns.'

'That's not surprising,' said the customer, and out she went.

'What did she mean by that?' Mrs East

27

wondered. But Amy couldn't think. And Brian had vanished.

'Perhaps it's too soon,' Amy said. Her teacher, Miss Wright, had told Class Three that the proper day to eat Hot Cross buns was on Good Friday.

'But other years we've always sold well the Saturday before,' Mrs East protested.

Nobody else came in for ages. Often by now, on a Saturday, a line of waiting customers stretched past the shop front and down the High Street. Amy would help her mother serve.

Mrs East smoothed her apron. 'Where are they all?'

Mr East was fetched.

Since five o'clock he'd been working hard. He bowled through the curtain, yawning. The shop went dark as a bus drew up and people flooded off.

'Do you see, Fred,' said Mrs East. 'Not one of them so much as looks in our window!'

Amy followed her mother and father out to the pavement. Two streams of people poured down the High Street, faster than the vehicles jammed in between.

The Easts went back inside. 'Amy,' Mrs East told her. 'Go and find out what's happening. Then come straight back and tell us.'

So off Amy went.

As she drew level with Pepper's something stung her leg. A funny noise came from under the potatoes. She snatched up the cover. There were Brian and Red giggling.

'Where are all these people going?' Amy asked.

'To the opening of the Sunny Stores. Andy Tearovski is coming to sign copies of his photo.' Red crawled out with Brian after him. 'You must have known.'

Amy shook her head.

'But everyone had a leaflet.'

Brian blushed.

Amy was angry. '*You* took ours because of Andy Tearovski, and never bothered about anyone else.'

Red's Uncle Archie came out of Pepper's. 'Buy our luverly ripe bernarners,' he shouted, but nobody did.

'We got to go now,' Brian told Amy. 'You tell Mum and Dad their customers will be along later.'

'They'll be lucky,' Red said. 'The Sunny Stores are selling just about everything.'

Amy turned to go back, but such a crowd was pressing forward she couldn't move.

'She'll have to come with us,' Red decided.

Amy was swept along in the stream that had grown to a great rushing river. After Jersey Joe's it poured to the left, into the road that led down to the end of the park. When she looked for Brian and Red, Amy found they had vanished.

The crowd stopped. Faces looked down on her. Voices spoke.

'Isn't that Amy at the Bakery?'

'Lift the little lass up. She'll never see anything from down there.'

So up she went, over the heads. Opposite was a big new shop, THE SUNNY STORES, with enormous glass windows and its own car park. Just stepping out of one of the cars was . . . Andy Tearovski. Amy recognised him from Brian's pictures.

Everybody cheered. Except Amy, who wriggled to be set down. Then she pushed her way out. Running down to the park gates she crossed the park, came out again in Church Way, up to the High Street and home.

'You've taken your time,' Mrs East said.

'I had to come the long way round.' When Amy had got her breath she told what had happened.

Just before dinnertime Brian returned with Red. They each had carriers with THE SUNNY STORES, STEEPLE FOLEY printed on the front. Inside were signed photos of Andy Tearovski.

'For every pound you spend,' Brian told them, 'you get two Hot Cross buns free.' He took a Hot Cross bun out of his pocket. 'I ate the other one.'

'And where did you get a pound?' asked his mother.

'Earned it.' Brian was so pleased with himself he didn't care about giving away secrets. 'Sortin' in Pepper's. So did Red.'

Mrs East turned to her husband. 'Did you hear that?'

But Mr East was picking up one of his own Hot Cross buns. He set it next to the one from

the Sunny Stores.

'Theirs isn't a patch on yours, Fred,' his wife told him.

'Can't say that until we've tested.'

Mr East cut up the buns and they all had a mouthful of each.

'I think yours is best, Mr East.' To be certain Red ate a whole one. 'Trouble is . . . who's going to buy yours when the ones at the Sunny

Stores are as good as free?'

After dinner Mrs East left Mr East and Amy in charge of the shop and marched off down the High Street. She plodded back with a grim expression.

'It's worse than we thought, Fred.'

Then Mr East went, and when he returned he didn't look happy either.

'What are we going to do?' Mrs East asked that evening. 'It's not only the Hot Cross buns. Their Simnel cakes are cheaper than ours. And they've hundreds of fluffy yellow Easter chicks . . . Oh, Fred!'

Amy and Brian glanced at each other. It was almost as bad as the time Mr East's oven blew up and burnt off his eyebrows. *They'd* grown back again . . . but would customers return?

'What *are* we going to do, Dad?' Brian asked.

'Sleep on it,' said Mr East.

So they did. And everyone woke up with a headache. Except Baby Roy, who was full of the joys of spring and hollered to be taken out.

Sometimes Mr East went with the children to the park on a Sunday morning. But today he'd planned the first baking of jammy hearts.

33

'What's the good, Dad?' Brian asked. 'If there'll be no customers to buy them?'

'That's enough of that talk.' Mrs East smoothed her apron. 'Folk are best kept busy with things weighing on their minds.'

'Not me,' Brian said.

'We all know you.' Mrs East filled a paper bag with Hot Cross buns for the ducks.

Just before they reached the alley Red popped out. Since he'd forgotten about breakfast he ate most of the buns. Then he and Brian ran off with Fruity, leaving Amy and Baby Roy behind.

As Amy fed the ducks she thought of all the buns left in the bakery. Not to mention the Simnel cakes and Easter chicks.

She pushed the pram to the end of the park and went out of the gate into the road which led to the Sunny Stores. The big car park was empty today. The new shop shut up tight.

'We must be the only people in Steeple Foley who haven't been inside,' she told Baby Roy.

Pressing her nose against the glass she saw long rows of freezers, shelves full of tins, cartons, bottles and packets. But when she stepped back . . . someone had drawn a heart in a dusty patch on the window.

Amy wheeled the pram up to the High Street, past the quiet Sunday shops. Pepper's was open, and Amy looked longingly at the daffodils.

'Take some for your mum,' Archie Pepper said.

Amy didn't have any money.

'With my compliments.' Archie took up a bunch, shook off the water and put them at the end of the pram.

'Where did you get those flowers?' Mrs East asked as Amy wheeled Baby Roy into the shop.

'They're a present. For you, Mum.'

Mr East, all floury from baking, came bowling through the curtain. 'Got a secret admirer, have you?'

'Only Archie Pepper, Dad.'

Mrs East handed the daffodils to Amy. 'I'll not accept favours, least of all from Pepper's. You can take these straight back.'

'No, Mum.'

'*What did you say?*'

'Oh, Mum! *Dad*! Never mind the flowers. If

the Sunny Stores can give things away for Easter, why can't we.

'What things?' her mother asked.

'Dad's new jammy hearts. How about . . . two free every time someone spends a pound?'

Mr East looked at Mrs East. 'We have a budding business woman here, my dear.'

Mrs East nodded. 'She's *my* daughter. And come to think of it, Fred . . . we could give away free yellow chicks with Simnel cakes an' all.'

At bedtime snick-snack noises came from Brian's bunk. He was cutting sticky tape to put up his new picture of Andy Tearovski. Baby Roy was going to sleep making pleased little murmurs. Everybody had been so good-tempered he hadn't had to cry all day.

The evening bus stopped outside. Amy fished under her pillow and brought out a jammy heart. Eating in bed was against the rules, but she reckoned she'd earned it.

3
Amy and the Diet

It was the first day of the summer term and
Amy had hurting knees. Mrs East felt her
forehead, and whispered to Mr East.

'Room Attic Fever?' Brian had sharp ears.
'What's that?'

'You get on and pack your schoolbag.' Mrs
East turned to her husband. 'I'm taking her to
the doctor, Fred. You'll have to mind the
shop.'

The doctor's was in Church Way so there
wasn't far to walk. But by the time they
reached the Midland Bank Amy's knees hurt
so much she had to stop. Her mother lifted
her up and sat her in the end of the pram with
her legs dangling.

'Phew! You're getting a weight, my girl.' Mrs East set off again.

Amy hoped nobody would notice them. But that was impossible in Steeple Foley.

Good morning, Mrs This. Nice day, Mr That. Mrs East never stopped. 'It's pains in her knees. Yes, a bit of a worry. We're off to the doctor now.'

Mr Pounce, the traffic warden, was lurking on the corner.

'Knees? Them's just growing pains. Had 'em myself when I was a nipper. Never stayed off school though. Or got pushed around in a pram. Mind, kids nowadays, driven about in motor cars.' He waved his book of tickets. 'Their mothers parking all over my yellow lines.'

'*His* yellow lines!' Mrs East rattled down Church Way. 'Who does he think he is?'

'A nasty old man,' Amy said.

'Now then, Amy. He *is* a customer.'

'Oh, Mum. Can't I get off now?'

'You'll have to,' Mrs East puffed. 'Pushing uphill is one thing, going down another.'

Amy slid to the pavement and began to

walk. 'Mum, my knees are better. I'm sure they are.' But by the time they were inside the doctor's they were hurting worse than ever.

'Rheumatic Fever?' The doctor looked up from examining Amy. 'No worry on that score, Mrs East. Just keep her off school for a couple of days.' He smiled at Amy. 'And no cream cakes.'

Cream cakes?

'You're getting a bit podgy, young woman.'

Then the doctor looked at Baby Roy and said what a fine *solid* little fellow he was growing. And that was that.

Although it was agony Amy insisted on walking all the way back.

Mr East was relieved to see them. 'Oh, Fred!' Mrs East burst out. 'Would *you* say as how she was podgy?'

To try and make herself look thinner Amy breathed in.

'Podgy?' Mr East repeated.

'That's what the doctor said.'

They all looked at each other. Then turned to the pram and the fine *solid* baby, fast asleep. Mr East even pulled back the curtain to examine Fruity.

'I suppose you could say we are all . . . on the generous side,' Mr East said slowly.

Mrs East smoothed her apron, then clapped her hands together, SMACK! Baby Roy woke up and stared at his mother in astonishment. 'We're *all* going on a diet.'

'Now hold on,' Mr East said. 'No need to act stupid.'

But Mrs East was determined. 'I'll not have it said that any of my family is *podgy*.'

The door opened.

CRACK!

Mr Pounce, six feet four and lean as a lamp-post, stepped into the shop rubbing his head. Over the years a head-shaped patch had been worn away by tall customers. The traffic warden bought his usual, a white thin-sliced and seed cake, then forgot to duck out again.

CRACK!

'There's one who doesn't need to slim,' said Mrs East.

'He could do with shrinking down.' Mr East bowled away to his kitchen.

Four customers came in, one after the other, and every one was slimming!

'No cakes,' said the first. 'I'm on a crash diet.'

Crash diet?

'Two slices of toast a day, and four oranges.'

Mrs East didn't fancy that. Four oranges per person, not counting Baby Roy. Sixteen oranges a day. Sixteen multiplied by seven? It was as bad as being at school, thought Amy. But . . . over a hundred oranges a week? Pepper's would think the Easts had gone barmy!

The next two customers were living on slimming biscuits so they could get into last year's summer dresses. They'd just come in to buy bread for their families.

Number Four, a stranger, asked for twenty wholemeal loaves.

'*Twenty?*' Mrs East was so surprised she forgot herself.

'To put in the freezer. I've only just moved in, and I'm stocking up. The Sunny Stores has most things, but I do like fresh-baked bread.'

Amy was sitting with Fruity on the stairs behind the curtain. While her mother went to the kitchen for more loaves Amy tweaked aside one of the strips.

The stranger was looking at everything. Bread, cakes, pies, biscuits. The wedding cake. Baby Roy.

'You dear little dumpling,' she told him.

When Mrs East returned the stranger pointed to the jammy hearts.

'Those look very good.'

Mrs East beamed. 'They're a new line of my hubby's. How many would you like?'

'Oh, I'm afraid I mustn't buy any. I'm on a diet.'

Amy watched her mother run her eye over the slim stranger. Then Mrs East smoothed her apron.

'What sort of diet might that be?'

'Just lean meat and fish. Fruit and vegetables. Good wholemeal bread, and plenty of exercise.'

When the stranger had gone Amy came out into the shop. 'That didn't sound so bad, Mum. Better than those others.' She rocked the pram. Baby Roy had liked the look of the stranger, and now she'd gone.

After school Sharon Bone came in for buns.

Sharon lived at the butcher's, and she was in Amy's class.

'Will you be back tomorrow?' she asked.

Amy shook her head. 'Wednesday.'

Sharon sniffed. 'There's a new girl sitting in your place.'

Amy frowned.

'She's a snob.' Sharon took a bite of bun. 'Nobody likes her,' she added with her mouth full.

After Sharon had gone Amy told her mother she felt like a bun.

'You look like one an' all.' Mrs East breathed in to make a better waist. 'No, Amy. I mean it. There'll be no more eating between meals.'

Mr East bowled through the curtain. 'That's a bit hard on a young 'un.'

Mrs East shook her head. 'I was young once, I'll have you know.'

'And a lovely young thing you was an' all.' Mr East caught his wife's eye. 'Not that you aren't still, my dear. Nice and rounded and . . . comfortable.'

'But I don't want to be, Fred,' Mrs East wailed. 'And Amy's not going to be neither.' She took some money from the till. 'There's a second-hand pair of scales down in Jersey Joe's window. And I'll pick up a weight chart from the chemist.'

When Brian arrived he helped himself to a doughnut. Amy watched the jam squirt out.

'Wipe your chin before Mum comes back,' she warned him. 'We're all going on a diet.'

It wasn't so bad to begin with. There was ham salad for tea, with tinned pineapple to follow. And although they were only allowed one slice of bread Mr East cut doorsteps.

'Don't think I didn't notice, Fred,' Mrs East told him.

Before they went to bed they stood on the scales. Even Fruity was heaved on, while Baby Roy was taken to the ones in the kitchen. Mrs East noted their weights to compare with the chart.

'This family is going to slim down if it's the last thing we do.'

'Probably will be,' Brian said gloomily. 'We'll all starve to death.'

He grumbled in bed. 'It's all right for Dad. He can top up while he's cooking. It's us that'll come off worst.'

Next day, in spite of breakfast, Amy felt hungry all morning. She kept going to look at the jeweller's clock. Never had time passed so slowly. And never had she been so glad to see her dinner.

In the afternoon the stranger appeared again, this time with a girl. A string bean of a girl who looked as though she'd been on a diet the whole of her life.

Mr Pounce was in the shop. When he saw the stranger a nasty look came over his face. Mrs East gave him his change quickly. Regular customer he might be, but a face like that could put a new customer off.

The stranger wasn't put off in the least. 'Thought you'd caught me, didn't you?' She waved a finger at the traffic warden.

Mr Pounce went tomato red. He straightened his neck until his head nearly touched the ceiling. Then he coughed in a most important manner.

'What a nasty cough, you poor dear,' the stranger told him.

The traffic warden was lost for words. Seizing his paper bag he strode to the door.

'Careful,' Mrs East warned. But . . .

CRACK!

'Poor thing,' said the stranger after the door had closed.

'Don't worry about him, my dear. He's a skull like cast iron, and a heart to match.' Realising she'd forgotten herself again Mrs East smoothed her apron and picked up a paper bag.

The string bean girl had been edging her way along the counter.

'Are those the ones, Mummy?' She pointed to the jammy hearts.

Her mother nodded. 'I'm having a little house-warming,' she told Mrs East. 'Just coffee and cakes. I'll take ten macaroons, ten lemon puffs, and thirty hearts, if you have them.'

Fifty cakes? Amy gave a gasp.

The curtain parted and the girl looked through. She stared in surprise at Fruity and Amy. 'Do you live here?'

Amy nodded.

'You lucky thing.' The girl slipped through the curtain. 'You're not *Amy East*, are you?'

Amy nodded again.

Fruity began licking the string bean girl's long legs.

'I suppose Sharon Bone's your friend.'

'Not specially.'

'When are you coming back to school?'

'Tomorrow,' said Amy.

Next day her knees felt quite better.

Mrs East wrote Amy a note to give to her teacher, Miss Wright.

'No extra helpings of school dinner now,' she told Brian and Amy.

As they passed the butcher's shop Sharon Bone came running out and tagged on to them.

Mr Pounce was lurking near the school gates. A red car pulled up and out popped a girl like a pip from a cherry.

'Hey!' Mr Pounce stepped forward, but the car had gone.

'That's her.' Sharon pointed. 'The snob.'

'No she isn't,' Amy said.

'How do you know?'

The new girl's name was Julia, and her surname was . . . *Stranger*! When the rest of the class saw Amy being friendly with Julia Stranger they were friendly too. All except Sharon, who was jealous.

After school she followed Amy and Julia across the playground calling them rude names. *Thin-shanks* and *Fat-drawers*. But she couldn't pester them for long because Mrs Stranger collected them *both* in her car.

'Feeling better now?' Mrs Stranger asked as Amy stepped on to the pavement outside the bakery.

'Yes, thank you.' Amy waved to Julia as the car moved off.

'You came home in style,' Mrs East said as Amy rushed in. 'I hope you said thank you.'

'Yes,' said Amy. 'I did.'

Tea was fish, with salad.

'We've never had salad with fish before,' Brian said.

'Well you have now.' Mrs East was in a bad mood because Baby Roy was playing up.

'You sure you're not starving that baby?' Mr East scrunched up a lettuce leaf.

'He's only cutting teeth, Fred.' Mrs East sent Amy to fetch the dummy.

Baby Roy took a long time to settle that night. And Brian talked. He talked about cream slices and jam doughnuts, chocolate cupcakes and strawberry tarts.

'Stop it,' said Amy. 'You're making me feel sick.'

Brian turned over in his bunk. 'How can you feel sick on flabby fish and lettuce?'

'We did have stewed rhubarb for afters.'

'Eurgh!'

There was a funny noise.

'What was that?' Amy asked.

'Haven't you ever heard a stomach rumbling before?'

At the weekend things grew desperate. There weren't even school dinners to fill up with. Brian went into Pepper's and did some sorting. He spent the money on popcorn.

'Popcorn's best,' he told Amy. 'It swells up inside you and fills all the corners.' He looked at her suspiciously. 'Have you been eating?'

Amy turned away, not wanting him to find out about the stale buns meant for the ducks.

Baby Roy was in such a temper he was allowed to suck his dummy all day. Then hungry Fruity invaded the shop and upset the tin of broken biscuits all over the floor behind the counter.

'Things can't go on like this!' Flour flew off Mr East in all directions.

Mrs East was stubborn. 'They'll have to, until we slim down.' But when they climbed on the scales again their weights had . . . *GONE UP!*

'We could try jogging,' Amy said. 'It's what my friend Julia's mother does.'

'Julia, how peculiar!' But after some motor-bikes had buzzed by Brian said, 'We'll try tomorrow.'

On Sunday morning Mr East came to the park. Red was there.

'We thought we'd go for a run,' Brian told him.

Mr East was feeding the ducks. 'Those knees of yours all right now, Amy?'

She nodded. It seemed years ago since they'd been hurting. 'Come on, Fruity. You've got to slim as well.'

'What's she talking about?' Red asked.

'Nothing special,' Brian said quickly.

They ran once right round the park. When they returned Red ate a stale bun. Then they went round again.

'What about *you*, Dad?' Brian puffed.

Mr East set off alone.

'You Easts have all gone barmy,' Red said.

Brian and Amy ate Sunday dinner, corned beef salad, stewed apple, and no seconds. They had nothing to eat all afternoon.

'And no drinking,' Brian warned Amy. 'Liquids weigh heavy.'

At last the weighing time arrived. They gathered round the scales, except Fruity, who wouldn't come out from under the table.

Mr East stepped on first. In spite of the run his weight had gone up. So had the children's!

'You've been eating secretly behind my back,' Mrs East accused them all.

'If only we had,' Brian said bitterly.

'You step on, my dear,' Mr East told his wife.

'Oh, Fred. I can't bear to!' She smoothed her apron bravely and . . .

Mr East burst out laughing. He couldn't stop.

'What is it, Fred?'

'You've hit the jackpot, my dear. *TWENTY STONE!*'

'She can't have, Dad,' said Brian. 'Can she?'

'On Jersey Joe's second-hand scales she has.'

They all went along to the scales outside the chemist's.

'There!' Mrs East said triumphantly. 'We *are* thinner!'

Gradually meals returned to normal, but everybody was careful not to overdo it. As Brian said to Amy, 'We're not going through all that again.'

4
Amy Moves in Circles

One day Amy came rushing home with a special question to ask her mother. She decided to lead up to it slowly. Baby Roy was teething and Mrs East had been very snappy lately.

'Mrs Stranger says our bread is the best she's ever tasted,' said Amy.

'Some people will say anything.'

'Mrs Stranger isn't like that,' Amy went on. 'And she's lived in all sorts of places. She's even lived in France.'

Mrs East sniffed. 'Nasty stuff, French bread. All crust, and hard as a rock.'

'Oh, Mum,' Amy said. It was no good, she'd have to come straight out with it. 'Can I go to tea with Julia?'

Mrs East was a long time answering. Then all she'd say was, 'We'll see what your father says.'

Mr East said, 'Why not? It won't hurt her to move in different circles. See how the other half lives.'

'As long as she don't come back with *ideas*.'

What were they talking about?

'If I let you go, Amy, you'll remember what I've taught you?' Mrs East said at tea-time. 'Say please and thank you. And don't wipe your fingers on the tablecloth. You'd better take a tissue to school to keep in your pocket handy . . . .'

'And the vacuum cleaner,' said Brian. 'Then you can pick up your crumbs.'

'Since you're so full of yourself,' his mother told him, 'you can take Fruity round the park. He didn't get his walk today.'

The reason for this was Baby Roy being out of sorts. Amy sat on the sofa with him looking at *Cakes and Pastries of the World*. She turned to the French pages.

'Cross aunts. Yummy.'

Baby Roy thought she said dummy, and

screamed until she fetched it.

'I wonder what we'll get for tea at Mrs Stranger's,' Amy said.

When Sharon discovered about the tea she was furious.

'*Snobs!*' she shouted, as Amy and Julia walked out of school and turned left at the gates. '*Amy East's gone la-di-dah!*'

They walked on, past all the roads leading off and the stretch of houses until they came to Foley Field. Then they turned into Foley Lane.

Here the houses were bigger and set back in the trees. Julia stopped by a gate in a tall hedge. On the other side of the hedge Mrs Stranger, in black tights, was standing on her head.

'What's she doing?' Amy whispered.

'Yoga. Doesn't your mother do it?'

Mrs East, in black tights, standing on her head in the bakery yard?

Mrs Stranger plopped down and stood the right way up. 'Who's this?'

'It's me, Mummy. And Amy at the Bakery.'

'Sorry, Amy,' Mrs Stranger said. 'I always take my contact lenses out before I do Yoga.'

'She's come to tea,' Julia went on.

They all walked round to the back of the house and into the kitchen. It was enormous. There were cupboards and gadgets galore, and the washing machine had a little room all to itself.

As they went upstairs to wash their hands Amy caught glimpses of other rooms. But when they reached the bathroom . . .

'Ooh!' Amy just couldn't look long enough.

'Hurry up,' said Julia. 'I'm starving.'

Amy washed her hands with soap that smelt of roses. She kept on smelling them all the way downstairs.

Their tea was on the kitchen table. Apple juice, wholemeal bread, apricot jam, banana yoghurt, and . . . Amy beamed.

'You like croissants, do you, Amy?'

She nodded, though not for anything would she tell Mrs Stranger she'd only ever *seen* cross aunts in *Cakes and Pastries of the World*.

'Your father doesn't bake them, does he?'

Amy shook her head.

'What a pity. Everybody eats croissants these days.'

Amy dropped a blob of jam on the table. It was lucky there was no tablecloth, just bare wood. And no washing-up either. The dirty things went into a dishwasher.

After tea Julia took Amy up to her room. This was so incredible that Amy could only sit on the furry rug and gape. It was like being in a toyshop!

'Daddy is always sending me things,' Julia told her.

'Doesn't he live here?'

Julia nodded. 'When he's not abroad. But that's not often. Sometimes I forget what he looks like.'

Amy tried to think how it would be with no Brian, Baby Roy, or Fruity, just her and Mum. Dad abroad, in France perhaps, learning how to bake cross aunts.

'Don't you get lonely?'

Before Julia could say Mrs Stranger called, 'Bring my cardy down for me, darling.'

They went into another bedroom. Amy was startled to see a little round girl following a tall thin one, before realising that side of the room was all mirrors. Julia slid one open.

Inside the cupboard were rows of dresses, tracksuits, clothes of every kind. Racks of shoes. It was like another shop. Julia pulled a fluffy black cardigan off a hanger.

When they went downstairs Mrs Stranger had the television on.

'Now bend,' said the lady on the screen. 'Stretch those muscles. Reach for the ceiling . . . twist . . . *bend*.'

And Mrs Stranger did.

Julia draped the cardigan over a chair like a

long lean cat, and they went into the garden to play. After that it was time to go home.

Amy burst into the shop and rushed upstairs. She couldn't wait to tell everybody everything.

'What did you have to eat?' Brian wanted to know first.

'Croissants,' said Amy, the way Mrs Stranger had said it.

'Oh my.' Brian made a gawpy face.

'Mrs Stranger says everybody eats croissants these days.'

'Does she now,' Mrs East said.

'We had apricot jam to go with them.'

'Yuck.' Brian didn't like apricots.

Amy took down *Cakes and Pastries of the World*, found the puffy golden horseshoes and laid the book on Mr East's lap.

'There, Fred. I told you she'd come back with *ideas*.' Mrs East set the table for to-morrow's breakfast, and sent Amy to start Baby Roy's bath.

'Oh, Mum! Do I have to?'

Mr East shut the book with a bang. 'Do as your mother says.'

Baby Roy's mouth went wobbly and he

began to cry. Amy snatched him up, set the bathwater running and began taking off his clothes. Since nobody else seemed interested she told Baby Roy instead.

'The bath was pink with gold taps. There were pink towels, pink everything. Even the soap and . . . oh, it was lovely at Mrs Stranger's.'

Baby Roy gurgled and kicked his legs.

Mrs East was in the doorway. 'There are lots of different sorts of people in the world, Amy.'

'I know, Mum.' She told her mother about the kitchen, and the great big garden.

'Like I said, Amy . . .'

But Amy didn't want to listen. She told about the room with the mirrors, and all the things Mr Stranger sent home.

That night she lay awake for ages. Baby Roy and Brian had gone to sleep a long time ago. It was dark now, and the headlights of passing cars made circles on the ceiling.

Amy had been moving in circles.

She thought again of Julia's room, and then she thought of *hers*. Barely room to move between the bunk beds and the cot. Three lots of clothes squashed into one small cupboard. All their toys in the drawer under the bunks. *What would Julia think of it?*

Two big tears burnt Amy's eyes and rolled off on to the pillow.

'When can I come to tea with you?' Julia asked a few days later.

'I'll see,' Amy said. But she didn't.

One day she walked home with Sharon.

'If you'll be my best friend,' Sharon said, 'I'll tell you a secret.'

'You don't know any secrets.'

'Yes I do. My sister Betsy's going to be Carnival Queen this year.'

'Really?'

Sharon nodded. 'And now I've told you're my best friend.'

Amy felt miserable. She didn't want Sharon for any sort of friend. She wanted Julia. But there were those circles.

Inside the butcher's Mr Bone was weighing mince. 'We'll play carnivals out in the yard, and I'll be Carnival Queen,' Sharon told Amy.

'I can't.'

'Why not?'

'I have to look after Baby Roy.'

'Bring him as well. He can be my little page boy.' Sharon stamped her foot. 'Fetch him!'

Amy shook her head. Sharon took hold of her by the shoulders. There was a knock on the butcher's window. Mr Bone was waving a mince-red finger. Amy wrenched herself free, and didn't stop running until she was safe inside the bakery.

Days went by. Miserable days.

At home Baby Roy set all their nerves on edge. Brian bought a second-hand torch from Jersey Joe to read in bed. Mr East was worrying again over the Sunny Stores. Mrs East worried about everything.

School was worse. Sharon was meaner than ever, and Julia couldn't wait to tear off home.

Just before half-term Mrs East said, 'Mrs Stranger was in today. She's worried about Julia. She isn't happy at school. And you've been funny. Aren't you two friends any more?'

Amy shrugged.

'Tell you what.' Mrs East smoothed her apron. 'You can ask her here to tea.'

'But, Mum, you said . . . .'

'I know.' Mrs East wiped Baby Roy's dribble and rocked the pram. 'Perhaps I said too much.'

'But, Mum. Suppose . . . .' Amy didn't know how to go on.

'Suppose she thinks you live in a dump?'

How could her mother know Amy was thinking an awful thing like that?

Mr East had been listening. All floury from the afternoon baking he bowled through the strip curtain. 'If she's a real friend, Amy, what will it matter about what you have or don't have? Friends don't bother with things like that.'

Amy waited until she and Julia were standing in the dinner queue next day.

'Will you come to tea with me tomorrow?'

For a terrible moment Amy thought Julia was going to say no, but then she nodded. 'All right.'

Sharon followed them up the High Street calling out names, but they couldn't be bothered with her.

There was a surprise waiting in the bakery window. Croissants. Or what was left of them.

'Customers have been queueing,' Mrs East said happily. 'Your father's pleased as Punch. I've saved one each for our tea.'

Baby Roy gurgled.

'And that's another thing,' Mrs East went on. 'He's cut his tooth, you'll be glad to hear.'

They peered inside Baby Roy's mouth to see the first white tip poking up. Then Amy led the way through the curtain. Fruity jumped up, overjoyed to see Julia.

On the stairs Julia tripped over a big bag of nappies and nearly fell down to the bottom. Mr East, all floury from the afternoon baking, came out from the kitchen. 'You all right, are you?'

As Julia nodded Baby Roy began to roar. He'd been left behind! Up he came, clinging to Amy and peeping shyly at Julia. When Amy had set him on the sofa she lifted down *Cakes and Pastries of the World* and showed Julia their pretend game.

After that Julia went and looked at St. Paul's Cathedral. She climbed up to Brian's bunk and saw his pictures and signed photo of Andy Tearovski. Then she looked in the toy drawer and out of the window. She saw the yard, and Mr East's kitchen with the big ovens and mixers. Julia was interested in everything.

When it was time to close the shop Mrs East let her turn the notice from OPEN to CLOSED and help tidy up.

For tea there was a big plate of bread and butter and croissants. Strawberry jam. Mixed cakes to follow. Tinned peaches. And a big bottle of fizzy lemonade.

Everybody was polite to begin with, but not for long. Brian wiped his fingers on the tablecloth when Mrs East wasn't looking. Mr East *boasted*.

'Very tasty, these cross aunts, though I say so myself.'

After tea Julia was allowed to help bath Baby Roy.

'I've never touched a real baby before,' Julia said. 'I wish he was mine.'

'You wouldn't sometimes,' Amy told her.

Baby Roy gave an enormous splash and soaked the pair of them.

Mrs Stranger came in her car to fetch Julia, who wouldn't stop talking.

'Oh my,' said Mrs East nervously. 'Giving away our state secrets. Your mother won't let you come again.'

'Yes she will.' Julia turned to her mother. 'Won't you?'

'If you're lucky enough to be asked.'

That evening Amy and Brian lay in their bunks. Baby Roy was fast asleep. Amy told Brian about Julia's father working abroad.

Cars buzzed past on the road outside.

'One day,' Brian said, 'I'll *drive* all over the world. Except for the bits where the sea is. I'll *jet* over them.'

Amy was happy just watching the circles.

5
Amy Meets Mister Nobody

When Amy went to Julia's for tea one Friday a strange boy was in the garden. He was sprawled on the ground reading *Treasure Island*.

'For the sixth time,' Julia informed Amy.

'Who is he?' Amy asked.

'Mister Nobody.'

Julia began digging for treasure, but all she found were earthworms, stones and some bits of old china.

'Hallo, Amy.' Mrs Stranger came bounding up in a jumpsuit all colours of the rainbow. 'What do you think of my Bobbydazzler?' She twirled around.

'It's lovely,' Amy said.

'Daddy sent it from Rome,' Julia told her.

'Put yours on and show Amy,' Mrs Stranger said.

'Do I have to?' Julia liked her old clothes best.

'I'm sure Amy would like to see it.'

When Amy nodded Julia shot her a disgusted look, but rose to her feet and headed for the house.

'Don't forget to wash your hands first,' Mrs Stranger called.

Julia's bathroom was still Amy's favourite place. She breathed in deeply, then pointed to a thing like a bald corn cob sitting on the pink bath.

'What's that?'

'A loofah.'

Amy had heard of a loafer, but . . . a loofer? 'What's it for?'

'Washing your back.'

Amy thought it must be horribly scratchy.

Julia was washing the bits of china she'd dug up. She dried them on a towel, then took them into her bedroom and laid them along the window-ledge. 'When I grow up I shall dig for treasure all over the world,' she told Amy.

'Let's see your jumpsuit,' Amy said.

It was black and white and golden brown, a floppy leopard. Amy tried it on, but she looked more like a round tabby cat.

When Mrs Stranger called them for tea they found Mister Nobody sitting on the stairs. Still reading. Amy had to squeeze past, but Mister Nobody didn't look up.

'*Who is he?*' Amy asked again as they went into the kitchen.

'My cousin. He's had chicken-pox, so he's come to stay for a bit to get over it.'

'But what's his real name?'

Mrs Stranger had overheard. 'Jonathan Anthony Barclay Wopping.'

'But everybody calls him Mister Nobody.' Julia helped herself to jam. 'So now you know.'

Did she? thought Amy.

After Mrs Stranger had called twice more Mister Nobody shuffled in. A gangly boy with chicken-pox patches and . . . *still reading*.

'One of these days,' Mrs Stranger said, 'you'll fall down a hole and never be seen again.'

Mister Nobody never even looked at Julia or

Amy. He just put out a hand and felt about for food.

'One of these days,' Mrs Stranger said, 'you'll pick up a plate and eat that instead.'

Amy wondered what her mother would think of him. He certainly hadn't bothered to wash his hands, say a single please or thank you, or even notice that they were there.

'Shall I tell you why he's called Mister Nobody?' Julia asked.

This was just what Amy did want to know, though she'd rather be told when he wasn't sitting opposite.

'He never does anything else but read. Apart from sleep and eat of course. And he wouldn't do them unless he had to. He isn't really here at all. That's why he's called Mister Nobody.'

The boy turned a page and spooned up yoghurt.

'Perhaps he'll put it in his car,' Julia said.

'Why, has he ever?' Amy whispered.

'No, worse luck. But he's always been the same, ever since he was born.'

'Babies can't read.' *Imagine Baby Roy reading while Amy pushed him round the park!*

'I bet Jonathan did.'

The name pierced Mister Nobody's skull. As he looked up with startled eyes Mrs Stranger bounded forward. 'Now then, Jonathan. This is Julia's friend Amy.'

Amy wondered whether she ought to say something special, like *Pleased to meet you*, even though she wasn't particularly, or perhaps *How do you do*? But before she could decide Jonathan Anthony Barclay Wopping, alias Mister Nobody, was safely back inside his book.

'Did you have a nice tea?' Mrs East asked when Amy went home.

'Yes thank you, Mum.'

Mrs East smiled and smoothed her apron. It was a rare treat to hear one of her family being polite without having to be reminded.

'It's your mum's birthday next week,' their father reminded them next morning when Mrs East had gone to open the shop. He gave Amy and Brian some money to buy her a present.

Brian said he was buying chocolates so Amy would have to think of something different.

Later on she pushed the pram down to Jersey Joe's.

'I want a birthday present for my mum,' she told him.

'Browse around,' said Jersey Joe in his wobbly voice. 'Be my guest.' He made a face at Baby Roy, who made one back.

Leaving them pulling faces at each other Amy turned the corner by the paperbacks and tripped over . . .

Mister Nobody! Flat on the floor, reading of course. Brian and Red came into the shop with Julia. Mister Nobody pushed the book he'd been reading back in the shelf and took out another.

'You're supposed to buy 'em, take 'em away, and read 'em at home.' Jersey Joe's voice wobbled all over the place. 'I gotta make a profit, you know.'

'I wasn't reading,' Mister Nobody said. It was the first time Amy had heard him speak. 'Only looking to see if I'd read them before.' He went all along the shelf. 'Read that. Read that. Read that. . . .' He'd read them all!

Then he walked through the shop bouncing off chairs and mattresses, and setting a table of

china rattling. When he reached the door he couldn't open it.

'*Don't push. PULL!*' said Jersey Joe.

'Who was that nutter?' Red asked.

Amy frowned at him. 'Julia's cousin.'

After Brian and Red had gone too, Julia helped Amy choose a china dish with roses all over. There was only a little chip on the edge. Jersey Joe rubbed off the price, wrapped the bowl in tissue paper and even found a box.

They hurried back to the bakery and Amy and Julia slipped upstairs to hide the box in the toy drawer.

Julia sat on Brian's bunk dangling her legs and cuddling Fruity. 'I wish I could live here.'

'You wouldn't like it really.'

'I would.' Julia jumped down. 'Best of all I'd like watching out of the window.' She did just that, then drew her head in again quickly. *'Come and see!'*

Stepping off the zebra crossing opposite Pepper's was Mister Nobody, closely followed by Brian and Red. They all disappeared inside the library.

'We'd better go too,' Amy said.

'Let him look after himself.' Julia climbed up Brian's ladder again.

But Amy knew what Brian and Red together could be like. 'Suppose he can't?'

'Oh, come on then,' Julia said.

Fruity followed them downstairs hopefully. 'We can't take you,' Amy told him. 'Dogs aren't allowed in the library.'

'Off again?' Mrs East asked as they crossed the shop.

At least Baby Roy was asleep in his pram.

'Only over to the library, Mum,' Amy said.

'Back in good time for dinner, mind.'

In the library it was just as Amy had feared. Brian and Red were doing everything they could to provoke Mister Nobody. Saying insulting things. Following him as he moved between the shelves. Pushing each other and banging into him.

After he came out Brian and Red followed, all the way to Foley Lane. Julia and Amy went too.

'About time,' Mrs East told Amy when she got back to the bakery. 'I could have done with a bit of help.'

Amy glared at her brother, slurping his dinner. *He* hadn't been told off.

'Pig-faced bully,' she whispered.

Baby Roy brought his spoon down, *wham!* Food spattered in all directions. Brian wouldn't stop giggling.

'I wish boys had never been invented,' Amy said.

On Sunday Mister Nobody was on the swings. *Still reading!* Brian and Red had more important things on hand though. Red had brought his skateboard, and Mr East was there. By impressing his father Brian hoped to get a skateboard of his own.

But on the following Friday . . .

'That nutter's still here,' Red told Brian as they came out of school. Mister Nobody, with an armful of books, was just ahead of them.

Brian turned round and said to Julia, 'What's your cousin's name?'

'Jonathan Anthony Barclay Wopping.'

'You shouldn't have told them,' Amy whispered. 'Now they're bound to do something.

Mister Nobody put on a sudden spurt and landed on the zebra crossing. When Brian and Red got there they had to wait for the traffic.

'You're not to *do* anything,' Amy told Brian.

Red laughed, the traffic stopped, and they all crossed over.

To Amy's relief Mrs Read, the librarian, was working in the children's section. Brian and Red hung about impatiently.

'If you boys can't settle you'd better go outside.' Mrs Read glanced at Mister Nobody.

'What a pity you can't behave like James here . . . .'

'James?' Red turned to Julia. 'I thought you said his name was Jonathan.'

When Mrs Read returned to her desk Mister Nobody followed her out with a pile of books.

'Thank you, James,' Mrs Read said as she took his ticket. And . . . 'Goodbye James,' as she handed it back again.

Mister Nobody was unlucky with the traffic this time. He had to wait to cross. Red and Brian caught him outside the butcher's. As they began to fight Mr Bone banged on his window. Sharon looked out from upstairs, and Mr Pounce came hurrying along.

'What's going on here?'

'It's *them*.' Sharon pointed triumphantly at Red and Brian. 'They stole that boy's library ticket.'

The traffic warden glared down. 'Hand it over.'

Instead Red ran. Brian ran. Mister Nobody ran. And so, of course, did Amy and Julia. Down the High Street, round the corner by Jersey Joe's, past the Sunny Stores and into the park. Right down to the lonely place where the river looped.

Under the trees Red stopped and flopped down, the library ticket still in his hand.

'Now then . . .' he gasped, wrestling with Mister Nobody who'd come to life in a surprising manner. 'Is your name . . . or is it not . . . Jonathan Anthony Bargy Whopper?'

'Barclay Wopping,' Amy said.

'Same thing.'

'No it isn't.'

Red passed the ticket to Brian. 'Well it's not James Bond, that's for certain.'

Julia stared.

'You're a criminal.' Brian waved the ticket at Mister Nobody. 'Giving in a false name.'

Julia turned on her cousin. 'Why didn't you use your own?'

'Because I'm fed up with it. Always having people laughing and calling me *Whopper. And* I'm fed up with being *Mister Nobody*. So when I had to fill in that form . . .'

'But why *James Bond*?' Julia asked.

Mister Nobody shrugged.

'Suppose Mrs Read had found out?'

'I don't live here. It's only temporary. I'm not doing any harm, Not like *them*.' He flicked a scornful glance at Red and Brian.

Oh no, thought Amy. Now they'll start fighting again. But instead Red said, 'There's a James Bond film on telly tomorrow afternoon.'

Mister Nobody looked interested, but Julia shook her head.

'You won't be able to see it, Jonathan. Mummy will be hogging the telly. There's tennis from Wimbledon.'

'Our set's on the blink an' all.' Red turned to Brian. 'It'll have to be yours.'

There was Amy, Julia, Brian, Red, Mister Nobody and Baby Roy. Not forgetting Fruity. *And* Mr East when he'd finished the afternoon baking.

After Mrs East had shut up shop they were still watching. But she couldn't complain on her birthday. And Mr East had baked a special cake with pale green icing, pink roses and thirty-three candles.

When the film was finally over the viewers discovered they were starving hungry. Mrs East invited them all to tea. Then she rang Mrs

Stranger and asked her too. Red ran home and returned with a bunch of red roses from Archie.

Mrs Stranger, in her Bobbydazzler, came with a bottle of champagne. Mrs East smoothed her apron and said, 'Thanks ever so. I'll keep it for later.'

'What about *now*, Mum?' Brian looked longingly at the feast.

'If we don't begin soon I'm starting on the baby.' Red took a pretend bite out of Baby Roy, who threw his spoon. It stuck in the jelly in Amy's dish with the roses showing through.

There were sandwiches and croissants. Sausage rolls, jammy hearts. Lemon puffs, chocolate cup-cakes. Raspberry ripple ice-cream with the jelly, and . . .

'Save a space for the birthday cake,' Mr East said as he lit the candles.

Baby Roy looked and looked.

Mrs East took a good deep breath and blew out all thirty-three candles. Everybody cheered. Including . . . *Jonny*! Because somehow that's who he'd become.

'*Jonny Wopping*,' Red said as they left to go home. 'I wouldn't mind a name like that. *Jonny*

Wopping, ain't that topping?'

Jonny had to stay James Bond in the library for the sake of Mrs Read.

The day he went home Amy, Brian and Red called at Julia's house to say goodbye. Nobody could find him. They searched the garden, and all the rooms.

'He's run off somewhere.' Red was disappointed.

'Wait a minute,' Amy said. 'I know where we haven't looked.'

Jonny was sitting in the bath, a book in one hand and the loofah in the other. But when he saw them he was pleased as anything.

After he'd dressed he ran out into the garden where they were digging for treasure. He joined in, and got dirty all over again.

6
Amy and the School Sports

The day before the School Sports, Amy came home to find Mr Pounce and Great-Gran Pepper arguing in the shop. And Baby Roy teething. *Again!*

'Oh, Amy!' Mrs East smoothed her apron. 'Take him for a walk, do.' She popped some stale buns into a bag for the ducks. 'My nerves won't stand any more.'

'You should try my job,' Mr Pounce said.

'*Sludge!*' said Great-Gran. 'Walking up and down all day, catching motorists. Call that a job?'

The traffic warden strode to the door, but Mrs East was too weary to warn him . . .

CRACK!

Baby Roy roared in his pram.

Amy ran to dump her schoolbag and fetch Fruity's lead. Ears flat and tail drooping he slunk from behind the curtain. Amy wheeled out the pram and off they went.

Fruity's ears and tail soon recovered. The ducks in the park polished off the buns. And Baby Roy looked sunny again.

'*Mumumdadablionaimeetootyfruity*!' he said.

'Baby Roy!'

Anxious to share this amazing event Amy turned for home. She'd almost reached the top of Church Way when Baby Roy flung out his woolly lamb. Amy put on the brake, ran into the road and . . .

SCREEEEEEEEECH!

When she dared to look up Amy saw on the side of the car, STEEPLE FOLEY SCHOOL OF DRIVING. PROP. C.R. ASH. Mr Ash was white as icing sugar, and so was his pupil . . . Miss Wright, Amy's teacher!

Attracted by the squeal of brakes Mr Pounce rushed round the corner.

'I might have known it. Learner driver. You can't stop there, on my yellow line!'

'*Oh no!*' Amy hurried home.

At least the four o'clock rush was over.

'Listen to this, Mum.' Amy tried to get Baby Roy to say his amazing word, but all that came out was . . .

'*Ono!*'

Mrs East sent Amy to set the table for tea. She had a Young Wives meeting to attend that evening, and Brian's and Amy's sports gear to get ready for tomorrow.

Next morning Amy and Brian loaded their schoolbags. Clean P.E. shorts and shirts. Clean white socks and plimsolls. Mrs East had been up until all hours. She couldn't attend the School Sports herself, but her children would look as smart as anybody's.

'Take care now,' she said as they set off.

'Good luck!' Mr East called from the kitchen.

As Red stepped out from Pepper's Great-Gran shouted, 'See you later, alligator.'

'*She's* not coming, is she?' Brian asked.

'Try stopping her,' Red moaned.

Sharon came out of Bone's kicking sawdust off her shoes.

'You won't win,' she told Amy. Julia was Amy's partner in the Three-Legged race this year. 'Her like a bean-pole and you a little podge.'

Amy and Julia had spent hours practising. On the school field in the dinner hours. Afternoons in the park. Round Julia's garden, where they'd fallen in the flowerbed and flattened the poppies.

'If I was your partner you might stand a chance,' Sharon said.

'Well you're not.' Amy hurried on to meet Julia, who'd come to school by car that morning.

Mr Pounce came racing down the High Street, but Mrs Stranger was safely away. She waved to him and called a cheery Good Morning.

As Mr Pounce stood glaring Miss Wright came along. Remembering what had happened in Church Way yesterday, Amy tugged Julia's arm. Just at that moment Sharon pushed her. Julia fell over, right on a sharp stone.

'Today of all days!' Miss Wright bent to blot Julia's knee. 'Why do you have to be so clumsy?' She was looking at Amy. 'Both of you need to *watch your step.*'

By the time Julia had been to the sickroom to be bandaged up properly it began to rain.

The Head sent a note round. Miss Wright read it out.

'*If the rain doesn't stop by the end of morning break School Sports will be postponed.*'

When the bell went it was still raining so they were sent into the hall. Sharon said that once when the weather was baking hot her sister Betsy had done a rain dance. Afterwards the rain had come down in buckets.

'So,' Sharon announced, 'I shall do a sun dance.'

Everybody watched because Sharon was a good dancer. She went to the Steeple Foley School of Dancing and had a red satin dress and tap shoes. Secretly Amy hoped she'd fall over to serve her right for pushing Julia. Instead the clouds outside rolled away and sun shone in the window.

Sharon said it was all due to her that Sports Day was saved. Nobody else said anything. How could you be sure of a thing like that?

By dinnertime Sharon was as full of herself as stuffed pork.

She turned up her nose in the dinner queue. 'Fish pie on Sports Day? *Eurgh!*' When she discovered there was macaroni pudding for afters she was rude to the dinner lady. 'I'm not eating that muck,' she said.

Amy and Julia went back for seconds to get their strength up.

'Some people,' Sharon said, 'will be so weighed down they won't stand a chance.' Then she told Jessie Owen, her partner in the Three-Legged, they were going to practise for the rest of the dinner hour.

Jessie went and hid in the toilets, but Sharon found her. She dragged her out and tied their legs together. 'Pick up your feet, stupid,' she ordered as they ran up and down.

'I bet poor Jessie wishes it was over,' Amy said.

'She shouldn't have let Sharon bully her into being her partner.' Julia stood up. 'I suppose *we* ought to practise. OW!'

Amy looked at Julia's leg. 'Who cares if we win or not?'

'I do,' said Julia. 'And so do you.'

They set off clumsily round the field. The grass was still a bit slippery and they had to dodge Sharon and Jessie . . .

BANG!

Miss Wright was marking out the course, and now there was a wiggledy line. 'I think it would be safer for everyone if you two dropped out,' she said.

By the end of the dinner hour the course had been marked, and chairs brought out for the spectators.

Julia waited by Miss Wright's desk. 'Please Miss Wright. My leg feels much better. My mother's coming specially, and if Amy and I don't run in the Three-Legged she'll be ever so disappointed . . . .'

'Oh very well.' Miss Wright began handing out team colours. 'The field is dry now but watch your footing, everybody. Teams will score six for a win, four for second, two for third.' She went to the staffroom to fetch the starting pistol.

Amy and Julia were Blues. Sharon and Jessie Reds. When two Yellows and Greens started an argument about who would win Sharon said, 'Don't be stupid. It'll be *Reds*, of course.'

'Who says?' somebody laughed. '*Old Nick?*'

Then Sharon began to dance. And somehow it was very scary. Every single person in Class Three watched in silence as Sharon danced and danced, up and down between the desks, until . . .

'Whatever are you doing, Sharon?' Miss Wright stood in the doorway.

'She's dancing to the devil, Miss,' somebody whispered.

Miss Wright went almost as pale as when she had nearly run over Amy. But before she could say anything the Head came bounding in to see if they were ready.

After they'd trooped out to the field nobody would go near Sharon, except Jessie and she couldn't help it.

By the time the Head's voice boomed through the loudhailer announcing the Under-Eights Three-Legged alot of races had been run. The score stood at Reds 44, Blues 38, Greens 20, and Yellows 16.

Sharon had won every race for which she'd entered.

While Miss Wright tied the runners' legs together a big black cloud moved over the sun. Amy heard Sharon say to Jessie, 'See you start off with your left, and don't you forget!'

'Yes, Sharon,' Jessie said in a frightened voice.

BANG! went the starting pistol.

A pair of Greens and a pair of Yellows fell over right away. Sharon and Jessie started well. So did Amy and Julia. They were just moving into the lead when Julia thought she saw lightning. 'Don't be silly,' Amy said. They'd nearly fallen and only just managed to stay on their feet.

'Out of the way!' came Sharon's voice. She and Jessie moved ahead. A yellow pair went past, but fell over. Two Greens went down at the same moment.

Drops of rain, as big as biscuits, began to fall.

'Don't look round,' Amy warned, but Julia couldn't help it.

'There's nobody else left on their feet!'

'We can't win anyway,' Amy said. Sharon

was reaching out for the tape. But . . .

Flash . . . CRASH!

Jessie screamed and went stiff as a post. Sharon lunged forward, and down they went. It was Amy and Julia who touched the tape.

After that the cloud moved off. The sun blazed down and dried out the grass. A freak of nature, everybody said. And the final score was . . . Blues 78, Greens 72, Yellows 64, and Reds 60.

To finish there was a Parents' Race. Mrs

Stranger, in her Bobbydazzler, came first. Great-Gran Pepper was last, though she got more cheers than anybody else.

'Thanks, dearie,' Great-Gran said as Mrs Stranger drove her home. 'I doubt I'd have made it on my pins.'

As Mrs Stranger drew in to the kerb Mr Pounce came running.

'Make yourself useful for once,' Great-Gran told him. 'Come round here and *fetch me out*!'

Amy and Julia got out as well. After Mrs Stranger had driven away Archie beckoned them.

'What's happened to our old lady? The way she's puffing anyone would think she'd been running a race.'

'She has,' said Amy. 'The Parents' Race.'

Archie went and told her off. 'You're a *great-grandparent*, Gran.'

'*Sludge*! I've still a pair of legs'—Great-Gran peered towards the pavement—'somewhere.'

Outside Bone's Sharon was trying to make Jessie go inside. Anybody could see Jessie didn't want to. She'd gone all stiff again. As Brian and Red came up behind them they lifted Jessie clean off her feet and carried her up to the bakery like a statue.

'You can stay here,' Amy told her. 'You'll be safe with us.'

Mr East, all floury from the afternoon baking, bowled through the curtain. '*Well then?*'

Amy and Julia hadn't been the only winners. Brian had won the Under-Tens Obstacle. And Red, who'd been practising secretly in his yard, had won the Sack Race.

They had a celebration. Amy, Julia, Brian, Red, and Jessie too. A cake each from the counter, and a bottle of fizzy lemonade to share.

When the shop was shut and only the Easts remained Amy took Baby Roy up for his tea. Afterwards, in the bath, he opened his mouth to take a drink of bathwater and . . .

'*Mum! COME QUICK!*'

Mrs East came running. 'Well I never. Another blessed tooth!'

That evening Mrs East opened her birthday champagne. The cork came out as loud as the starting pistol at the Sports. It hit the ceiling and frightened the life out of Fruity. Amy and Brian each had a sip of champagne, but didn't think much of it.

When they were lying in their bunks Amy said, 'Sharon Bone did a terrible thing. She danced to the devil so she would win.'

'It didn't work though, did it?'

'Suppose it had?'

'Suppose you shut up and go to sleep.'

A few weeks later Miss Wright passed her driving test. But Baby Roy never said his *tootyfruity* word again.

7
Amy and the Carnival

It was a hot July evening. The church clock had just chimed eight, but voices and traffic still blew in the window. And Baby Roy was still awake.

'*Ummummummummumm. . .*' he buzzed.

There was a noisy burst of cheering outside. Amy looked anxiously in the cot, but Baby Roy had gone to sleep clutching his woolly lamb.

'Brian,' said Amy. 'What's happening?' But Brian was reading.

Mrs East pushed open the door. 'Are you two still talking?'

Chance would be a fine thing, Amy thought.

Her mother pulled up Baby Roy's blanket. Then she came and covered Amy.

'Oh, Mum. It's too hot!'

When Mrs East opened the window Amy could hear music.

'What is it?'

'The Morris Dancers practising at the Pig and Whistle.' Mrs East smoothed her apron. 'There'll be no more peace in Steeple Foley until the Carnival is over.'

A bus pulled up and voices floated out of the windows and into the bedroom.

'What do you want?' Mrs East asked. 'Air and noise, or heat and quiet?'

'Air,' said Amy.

'Quiet,' said Brian.

So Mrs East left the window halfway.

After she'd gone Amy thought about the Carnival. The big procession through the town. Not only the Morris Dancers, but floats as well. Cubs, Brownies, Boys Brigade, Young Wives, the Darts Team at the Pig and Whistle, the Steeple Foley School of Dancing . . . .

This year the theme for the floats was to be 'The World of Films'. And tomorrow at Brownies they'd vote for *their* float.

'I'm fed up,' Julia grumbled after she'd

called for Amy next day. 'All we ever do at Brownies is play the same old games and sing the same old songs.'

'Today will be different,' Amy said. 'You'll see.'

First they voted, and the film that won most votes was 'The Wizard of Oz.' Next came auditions.

Carrie Ash was just right for Dorothy. Julia made a perfect Scarecrow. Jessie Owen went stiff with fright, then found she was to be the Tinman. Amy couldn't decide whether to be pleased or not at being chosen for the Cowardly Lion.

Sharon said she could have played any of the parts standing on her head. She needn't bother though, because she'd be on the best float of all. The Steeple Foley School of Dancing. *And* her sister Betsy was Carnival Queen.

Who cared?

On Saturday Mr Pounce came into the bakery . . .

CRACK!

'Crazy time is here again.' He rubbed his head. 'Cars parked any old where. Little children getting themselves lost. I just can't bear to think of next Saturday.'

'It's only once a year,' Mrs East protested as she put Mr Pounce's seed cake into a paper bag.

'*Pah!*' Mr Pounce headed for the door.

'Look out!' warned Mrs East, but . . .

CRACK!

Amy came out from behind the counter where she'd been practising being a lion.

'*Eurrgh, eurrgh*! Imagine living on seed cake and getting like Mr Pounce. *Eurrgh, eurrgh!*'

Baby Roy began *Eurrgheurrgh-ing*, and Fruity whined behind the curtain.

Mrs East smoothed her apron. 'My nerves won't stand any more. Get up off that floor, Amy, and take them for a walk, do.'

'What, your nerves?' Amy didn't wait for an answer. After she'd fastened on Fruity's lead and sat Baby Roy up she wheeled out the pram.

The park was full. And everybody was talking about the Carnival.

By keeping her ears open Amy discovered that the Darts Team of the Pig and Whistle were building a giant spaceship for 'Star

Wars'. The Steeple Foley School of Dancing's float would be 'The Snowman'. And the procession would be led by the famous Townsville Drum Majorettes.

Mrs East sang as she bathed Baby Roy that evening. 'The hills are alive . . . .' Yes, the Young Wives had chosen 'The Sound of Music'.

Amy and Brian looked round the door. Baby Roy was drinking his bathwater again.

Brian was very pleased with himself. The Cubs were doing 'Tarzan of the Apes'. He was to be a lion too, but a brave one.

Mr East was inventing. Every year he made a special cake for the bakery window. After the Carnival was over it was given to the Steeple Foley Old People's Home.

'Dad?' said Brian. 'Calling Dad. Are you receiving me? Over.'

'How about this?' Mr East waved a floury hand. 'A white iced square. Chocolate footsteps across the icing. And Charlie Chaplin, all in black, twirling his stick.'

'Ace, Dad,' Brian said, and Amy agreed.

On Sunday the flags went up across the High

Street. The big bunting with WELCOME TO STEEPLE FOLEY CARNIVAL stretched from the top window over Pepper's to the one above the Pig and Whistle.

Mrs Read came riding up the High Street, jumped off her bicycle and let herself into the library. Then she went up to the storeroom and dropped down the end of a row of flags. Mr East took it across the street, fixed it to a long pole and pushed it up the bakery wall. Mrs East leaned out, hooked it in and fastened it to the end of the bunks.

The morning of the Carnival Amy woke early. Brian and Baby Roy were still asleep. She crept to the window.

'Look!'

Brian woke. 'What's up?'

'It's all misty,' Amy whispered. 'The little flags are soaking wet and I can't see farther down than Pepper's.' She looked the other way.

The jeweller's clock was a castle in the air. Below it loomed a giant monster which stopped, panting, outside the bakery. Then it puffed off down the High Street to lose itself under the bunting.

'Buses are running, so it'll be all right,' Brian said.

'But suppose it stays like this all day?'

As Fruity nosed his way in Amy looked in the cot. Baby Roy had turned himself upside down, and back to front!

'How did he do that?' she asked Brian.

'He thinks he's a lion.'

Mrs East looked in the door and gave a scream. Mr East, all floury from the early baking, came running.

'Just look at him, Fred. He'll be crawling next!'

A terrible noise came out of the mist.

'*Fred! What was that?*'

'Only Archie practising his Tarzan cry,' Brian said.

By the time they'd finished breakfast the sun was out. And as the church clock struck nine the last of the mist vanished. Amy turned the notice from CLOSED to OPEN, and Mrs East unlocked the door. The shop filled up at once.

'It's going to be a beautiful day,' said the first customer.

Mrs East smoothed her apron. 'And a busy

one.' The bakery was supplying the cakes for the Carnival.

The queue outside grew longer until it stretched all the way to Pepper's. There hadn't been such a queue since before the coming of the Sunny Stores. After it had gone there was still a crowd looking at the Carnival cake in the window.

After dinner Brian and Amy ran into the bedroom to change. Jersey Joe had come by a load of animal costumes, and Brian's and Amy's were exactly the same.

As they went downstairs Mr Pounce came hurrying into the bakery . . .

CRACK!

'Serve me first please.' He rubbed his head. 'If I'm not there those floats will get in a tangle, as sure as drivers park on yellow lines.'

Fruity growled behind the curtain, and out jumped two lions. Baby Roy gave a scream of joy.

Next came Mr East, not floury for once, but polished and shiny. He beamed proudly at Mrs East stepping out from behind the counter in a dirndl dress and new white apron.

Mr Pounce bowed and said gruffly, 'Very nice.'

Mrs East blushed and forgot to warn him . . . CRACK!

'See you later, Fred,' Mrs East told her husband. 'And don't forget the extra doughnuts.' Mr East was closing the bakery early and taking Baby Roy to the Carnival.

Amy, Brian and Mrs East hurried up to Church Way, where the floats were gathering.

First came the Boys Brigade Band. Next the Townsville Drum Majorettes. Followed by Betsy Bone, the Carnival Queen, on a throne in a flower-filled trailer. The floats came in all sizes. Big ones pulled by tractors and trucks. Smaller ones behind vans and cars. Mr Pounce tore about getting them all in line.

Mrs Read rode up. She wore an old leather flying cap, Air Force jersey, and trousers tucked into her socks. Fixed to her handlebars was a pair of wings.

'Which of you two is the "Wizard of Oz" lion?' she asked.

Amy swung her tail. She liked nobody knowing who she was. Brian swung his tail too.

'Well whoever it is, look sharp. Your float's in place.'

'I want to look at the others first,' Amy told Brian. 'It's the only chance we'll get.'

They ran from one to another, looking at people they knew transformed into film stars. Ivor Pollock, the fishmonger, was Superman, and the leader of the Pig and Whistle Darts Team, Darth Vader.

The Boys Brigade Band started tuning up. 'Walking in the Air' floated out from 'The Snowman'. Followed by rock music, pop music, and old-fashioned slop music, as all the other floats joined in. The Morris Dancers jingled their bells.

'What a row!' Brian said.

A Boys Brigade bugle blasted out.

'We'd better get on our floats now.' Amy ran, tripped over her tail, picked it up and . . .

'GOTCHER!'

She rose into the air. Then she was squeezed backwards through rails, and dumped on a saw-dust floor. Archie Pepper, shining with suntan oil, took hold of a rope hanging from a pretend tree. 'I'm not your lion,' she tried to

say, but there was too much noise.

As the float jerked forward somebody poked Amy in the back. 'Come on, Easty, you dozy old lion. *Roar*!'

Amy crawled to the front of the float. 'The Wizard of Oz' was directly ahead, she knew. Jumping up she clung on a rail to see over the driving cab. The Brownies had their lion!

THUMP!

Someone had pulled her down by her tail. A crocodile spoke in her ear. 'You're a lion not a tiger, Easty.' Soon they'd turn the corner into the High Street. 'Outside the Midland Bank you start.'

START WHAT?

If only Brian had told her. All she knew was that Tarzan's lion was brave.

Amy felt herself dragged backwards. If her poor old tail had much more pulling it would come right off! Sawdust flew up into her nose. She sneezed.

'Roar, Easty. *Roar!*'

'Just a minute,' she tried to say, but an ape had jumped on her. He shook her by the shoulders. All her teeth were rattling. The truck must have drawn level with the bakery because just for a moment Amy saw her father holding up Baby Roy. Then . . .

'*AAAROOAAAROOAAAROOAAAROOAAA. . .*'

Tarzan of the Apes swung on his rope straight at Amy. She ducked. Tarzan flew over the top and hit his head on a rail . . .

THUD!

'*Brian!*' A gorilla was shaking her, but he had Red's voice. 'You wally. Archie was supposed to ride on your back, not knock himself out!'

Amy pushed the gorilla over. '*I'm not Brian!*'

Fortunately the Cubs were well up in First Aid. By the time the procession had left the High Street and turned into Foley Field Tarzan was sitting up and taking notice.

'What happened?' He felt the rising bump on his forehead. 'Last thing I remember was heading for the lion. Did the rope break?'

'No, Archie,' Red said. 'We got the wrong lion.'

The Boys Brigade Band marched round the edge of the field behind the sideshows, and the floats bumped to a halt one by one.

First off the Brownies' was Brian.

'I was never found out,' he roared. He ran round the Cubs' float punching everyone. Being cowardly had been a strain. Then he remembered Amy. 'Archie didn't hurt her, did he?'

'Not exactly,' Red said.

When Betsy Bone heard about Tarzan's

accident she forgot about being queenly. Tearing along, her crown in one hand and her sceptre in the other, she flung herself at Archie.

'Oh, pet!' Betsy cried. 'Are you all right?'

Archie let out a Tarzan cry to show how all right he was. Then he went off to win her a coconut.

The floats stood abandoned like empty ships. Snowflakes were sucking iced lollies, and drum majorettes tucking into doughnuts.

Amy, Julia, Carrie and Jessie walked round the field looking at everything. Inside the Lost Children's tent they found Mr Pounce drinking tea. The only child was Baby Roy, and he wasn't lost. Just waiting while Mr East delivered the extra doughnuts to the Refreshments Tent.

Red and Brian put their heads inside. 'Guess who's driving round the field?'

'*Driving?*' Mr Pounce hurried outside.

It was Andy Tearovski, come to sell autographs in aid of charity.

On Sunday afternoon Mr East took the Charlie Chaplin cake out of the window and Archie drove them in his van to the Old People's Home.

Great-Gran cut the cake, '*Sludge*! This icing's like rock!'

Archie in his Tarzan rig, and Betsy the Carnival Queen, handed round cups of tea and cake. The icing might have gone hard but the cake was safe and soft inside.

After they'd driven home Mrs Read rode up the High Street on her bicycle. She climbed the library stairs to the storeroom. Mr East untied the row of flags from the bunks, and Mrs Read hauled it in through her window.

'That's that.' Amy looked out, remembering the misty mysterious morning. The Carnival was over for another year but weeks of holiday stretched ahead. All the time in the world . . . .

8
Amy's Summer Holiday Visitors

Julia was going to stay with her cousin Jonny while her mother went abroad.

'I don't want to,' she told Amy. They were on the swings in the park. Baby Roy was asleep in his pram and Fruity was keeping an eye on the ducks.

'Stay with us instead,' said Amy.

'Could I really? *Yes please*!' Julia jumped off her swing. 'I'll go and ask Mummy right away.'

'Hold on,' Amy said. 'I have to ask *my* mum first.' She fetched the pram. 'We've never had anyone stay before.'

'Never?' Julia couldn't believe it.

'There's no room, is there?'

This was exactly what Mrs East said.

It was lucky that Great-Gran Pepper was in the bakery collecting her bread. 'Just the two of you and three nippers?'

'Six in all.' Mrs East nodded at the pram. '*And* there's Fruity.'

'*Sludge*! Babies and dogs don't count!'

'Pardon me.' Mrs East smoothed her apron. 'Babies and dogs can take up a great deal of room.'

'I've packed fourteen humans in your space, dearie, an' all of 'em Peppers.' As Great-Gran toddled out Brian came in.

'You wouldn't mind if Julia came to stay, would you?' Amy asked him quickly.

Brian stared. 'She's not having my bunk.'

Mr East, all floury from the baking, bowled through the curtain. 'How about the sofa?' he suggested.

Julia nodded. 'I'd *love* to sleep on the sofa.'

Then there was only Mrs Stranger to ask, and she didn't need much persuading.

The day Julia came began much the same as any other. She and Amy pushed the pram to the park, fed the ducks, had a swing, played with Fruity and pottered back to the bakery.

Julia was used already to dinners and teas at Amy's, but supper was different.

So was going to bed on the sofa. Waking the next morning to find Fruity licking her face, and Amy in her pyjamas carrying the baby. Mr East, all floury from the early baking, wanting his breakfast. Mrs East in her nightdress asking, 'You slept comfortable? Didn't fall out in the night?'

'Oh Mum,' said Amy. 'Stop fussing, do.'

She and Julia took Baby Roy and put him on the bottom bunk, while Fruity scrambled up to the top.

'Great-Gran Pepper should see us all now,' Julia said.

'You must be joking.' Brian came down the ladder and went to get dressed in a quiet place where no one could see him.

After breakfast Julia turned the shop notice from CLOSED to OPEN the moment the church clock struck nine. She couldn't wait to serve a customer.

While Amy was dressing Baby Roy, Brian came rushing up the stairs. *'Don't let Fruity out!'* The door banged behind him.

Amy hurried down and strapped Baby Roy quickly into his pram. Fruity barked and barked upstairs.

'Whatever is going on?' Mrs East asked.

Amy and Julia went to find out.

Brian and his father were in the yard. 'We've another visitor,' Mr East said.

'It's a racing pigeon!' Brian lay flat on his stomach and looked at the rings on the bird's legs. 'How are pigeons raced, Dad?'

'They're put in crates and taken by lorry, sometimes as far as five hundred miles.'

Brian whistled.

'Then they're released to fly home. Usually it only takes a few hours, but bad weather can blow them off course.'

'Is that what's happened to this one?' Julia asked.

'Perhaps.'

'Poor thing,' Amy said. The pigeon looked at her with its round bright eyes. 'Is it hurt, Dad?'

Mr East spread its wings and felt them gently. 'Nothing wrong there. All we can do is let the bird rest. Bring it some water, Amy.

Brian, go and fetch birdseed from Pepper's.'

Red came with the birdseed, to which Mr East added some wheat and oats. The pigeon, however, neither ate nor drank. It just stayed quite still in the middle of the yard, and looked at them.

All day long they took turns keeping watch. And that night Mr East put the bird in a cardboard box and carried it indoors to leave by his open bedroom window.

The next morning the pigeon was still there.

Mrs East was crotchety. 'Not a wink of sleep have I had all night, thinking about that blessed bird. And whether it would rain, or a burglar climb in.'

For another whole day the children took turns looking after the pigeon. That evening Mr East assured his wife, 'It'll fly at dawn.'

But it didn't.

Next morning Mrs East had black rings under her eyes. She smoothed her apron six times in a row. 'Something will have to be done!'

'What were you thinking of, my love?' Mr East raised his floury eyebrows. 'Pigeon pie?'

Julia looked shocked, but Amy nudged her. 'It's only one of Dad's jokes.'

'We could do without *them* today, thank you,' Mrs East snapped. Brian was picking at his breakfast, a most unusual sight. 'It's upsetting us all!'

'It's not the pigeon, Mum.' Brian went red. Then he took a handful of money from his pocket and poured it on to the table.

Mrs East's eyes popped. 'Wherever did you get all that?'

'Earned it, towards my skateboard. I can have it, can't I, Dad?'

'But your birthday's only the day after tomorrow,' his mother said.

'I'll go without a birthday tea or anything. And I'll earn some more, sorting in Pepper's. I'll sort all day and night *all through the holiday*, if only I can have a skateboard of my own,' Brian pleaded. He was still pleading when the church clock chimed . . .

NINE!

And the shop wasn't open!

In the rush to get downstairs the pigeon and the skateboard were forgotten. But later on, in the park, Julia said to Amy, 'If we did some sorting we could give the money we earned to Brian. It could be our birthday present for him.'

After dinner Mrs East decided that Baby Roy would be cooler behind the counter than outside in the heat. Amy and Julia followed Brian along the alley.

As Red opened his gate a smell of rotten fruit came out.

'*Pooh!*' said Julia. '*What a pong!*'

Great-Gran was in her sentry-box. 'We got no time for fusspots here.' She pointed at Julia. 'Who's she?'

'My friend Julia,' Amy said. 'And she'll work as hard as I do.'

First they sorted cherries. When Great-Gran dozed they ate a few, and had a pip-spitting competition with Brian and Red.

Great-Gran woke and caught them. 'Work?' she said. 'You don't know the meaning.'

Next came plums, and the bad ones were horrible. Their fingers sank into mouldy mess.

'That'll learn you,' Great-Gran cackled. But after a bit her eyes closed and her head dropped.

Brian grinned. 'Now we'll have some peace.'

'Trouble is, she's got a terrible suspicious mind,' Red said. 'When she wakes she'll say we've been skiving.'

'Wake her up then.'

Red wriggled Great-Gran's knobbly knee. Nothing happened. '*Sludge*!' he said in the old lady's ear. She lolled sideways and her mouth fell open.

'Perhaps she's died,' Brian said.

Red shook her head. 'Not her. She'd wait until she'd finished sorting.'

'People don't die just when they want to,' Julia said.

Amy remembered Brownies' First Aid. 'Put a mirror in front of her mouth. If it steams up she's still breathing.'

But nobody had a mirror, and . . . *Suppose it didn't?*

Red rushed to the shop and brought back Archie.

'She's never still in that box!' Archie leaned over, then pulled the old lady gently to her feet. Her knees sagged and her arms flopped. Amy could hardly bear to look. Then . . .

'It's not my bedtime,' Great-Gran said faintly. 'Put me back!'

'It's too hot,' Archie told her. 'You're coming indoors.'

First she made Archie pay the sorters their earnings. Then she went.

Red tried out the sentry-box for himself.

'Phew! Talk about an oven!'

Julia pointed to the shelf above his head. 'What's that for?'

'Gran to keep her knick-knacks. Except she can't reach, so she doesn't.'

'It would be all right for a pigeon though.'

They went and told Mr East, who had a word with Archie. Later they carried the sentry-box between them out from Pepper's and along the alley.

It looked very strange in the middle of the bakery yard.

'Whatever does old Gran Pepper want with a sentry-box?' Mrs East demanded.

'It's not a real one, Mum,' Brian said. 'Just something Archie built, so she doesn't feel the draughts when she's out in the yard.'

'At her age she should be indoors.'

'But she likes it out there, Mum.'

So fortunately did the pigeon. It took to the high shelf as though it was home. There it would be safe from cats. And Mrs East could have a good night's sleep.

She slept so well she forgot to wake in the morning. So did Amy, Baby Roy, Julia, and Fruity. Perhaps it was the heat. Only Mr East, used to hot ovens, crept out of bed at five o'clock as usual to set the dough rising.

'Well I'm blowed.' He shook his head, all floury from the baking, when he returned for his breakfast at eight o'clock. 'And that blessed pigeon out there still asleep an' all!'

'Dad?'

Amy stood in the doorway rubbing her eyes. Fruity woke. Julia woke. Baby Roy and Brian woke. Mrs East last of all, but when she did . . .

PHEW! WHAT A RUSH THERE WAS THEN!

At least they managed to open the shop on time, though the children were still in pyjamas.

CRACK!

Mr Pounce stood rubbing his head. 'What's this?' Hastily Mrs East tied and smoothed her apron. 'Children not dressed at nine o'clock?'

'It's their holiday,' Mrs East said shortly.

'They're always on holiday if you ask me . . . .' A car stopped outside on the yellow line. The traffic warden dashed to the door.

'Careful,' Mrs East warned. But . . .

CRACK!

As the children went giggling up the stairs Red came to say that sorting was off. Great-Gran was taking a rest. They could all go along and help Archie sort later when the heat of the day was over.

It was sweltering already.

'A good day for a picnic in the park,' Mr East said.

So Mrs East let Julia serve while she filled some bags with pies and buns. Amy got Baby Roy ready. Brian went out for a large bottle of lemonade, and Red brought apples and oranges. They piled everything on to the end of the pram, and off they went.

When they returned to the bakery they found the sentry-box in the shade, and the pigeon walking up and down. It pecked at its grain, and drank from the water bowl on the ledge.

'It's happy now,' said Amy. 'I wish it could stay.'

Mr East shook his floury head. 'Somebody somewhere is waiting to see it fly home.'

When Baby Roy had gone to bed the children went to help Archie sort. They earned a bit more towards the skateboard, but would they ever have enough?

Nobody overslept next morning. As Amy took Baby Roy to wake Julia a loud clanging rang through the bakery. Brian came running, and so did Mrs East. Amy pointed.

'*Look! LOOK!*'

'That blessed bird!' said Mrs East.

The sun gleamed on its blue-grey wings as it circled to get its bearings. For a moment Amy saw its eyes, then it turned to the north, growing smaller and smaller, until . . .

'It's gone,' said Julia.

Amy felt a bit like crying, but Mr East came bowling in, flour flying in all directions. 'You saw it, did you?'

'And we heard you.' Mrs East smoothed her nightdress.

'There was no time to warn you, my love.

Only to bash some bread tins together.'

Brian let out a yell that was even louder. There was a parcel on the breakfast table, so big it almost covered the top!

'Happy birthday,' Amy said, and so did everyone else.

Brian took his new skateboard to the park and practised all day. When the afternoon baking was finished Mr East went along to watch.

After the shop was shut they had birthday tea. Red was invited, and there was a surprise skateboard cake, with nine candles.

Later they put Baby Roy in the pram and went back to the park again. This time Mrs East came too. Mr East sat her on a suitable seat. 'When you see how well he rides, my dear, you can stop worrying about broken bones and him landing in the river.'

The first thing Brian did was fall over, but afterwards he gave a display which had Red looking envious.

Of course there had to be some rules. *Only riding in the park. No dangerous stunts.*

'No anything exciting,' Brian grumbled before he went to sleep that night.

'You've got it, haven't you?' Amy asked.

'Yes,' said Brian. 'And thanks for doing the sorting and giving me the money.'

'I wasn't the only one,' Amy told him.

So Brian slid down the ladder, crept into the living room, and thanked Julia as well.

When Mrs Stranger walked into the bakery Julia couldn't stop talking. She didn't tell about the pigeon, sorting in Pepper's or Brian's birthday, but all the customers she had served. 'Miss Wright and Mrs Read. Ivor Pollock. Betsy Bone. The Bank Manager . . .'

Mrs Stranger invited Amy to stay with Julia. She made up another bed in Julia's room. Amy enjoyed waking up to all Julia's things, but best was having foamy baths and coming out smelling beautiful.

Some part of every day Amy and Julia went up to the bakery to help Mrs East.

In Pepper's Great-Gran sat on a chair in the shop and bossed the customers. But when the air grew fresher she returned to the sentry-box in the yard, to Archie's relief.

The first yellow leaf spun off the trees by the river. Soon it would be school again.

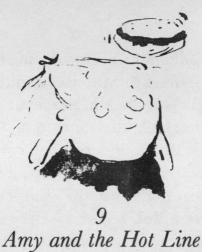

9
Amy and the Hot Line

Worry was loose in the High Street. It hung about the little shops like a lost dog. Worry, worry, worry. And the cause of it all? Leaflets. CUT-PRICE AUTUMN ATTRACTIONS. The Sunny Stores were after customers again.

The children had worries of their own.

Amy worried about her new teacher, Mr Hardy. 'I don't think he likes me,' she said as she lay in her bottom bunk.

Brian, in the top bunk, was worried his torch battery would run out before he'd finished his book.

'*I* won't like you if you don't let me get on . . . *Oh!*'

Darkness reigned. Apart from headlights,

and nobody could read by them.

Next morning Brian still wouldn't talk to Amy. Mr East sat at the breakfast table like a floury ghost. Baby Roy was throwing things. Fruity nipped her.

Amy turned on the telly.

'You can switch that off.' Mrs East didn't approve of breakfast televison. There was quite enough to be got through without watching other people's doings. 'Come along now.'

All Amy had managed to see was an advertisement for a burger.

For some reason the burger stayed in her head all day. She couldn't seem to get rid of it. Whenever she looked up from her classroom desk there it was, floating in the air in front of her. Just before home time it floated over the head of Mr Hardy.

'Are you in a trance, Amy? Or are you thinking?'

The class giggled.

Sharon poked Amy in the back. 'Wake up, Fatbum,' she said loudly.

The class giggled again and waited to see what Mr Hardy would do. He kept Sharon in for ten minutes after school.

Julia walked home with Amy. They spent so long looking in Jersey Joe's window that Sharon caught them up. But just before she reached them . . . CRACK! Sharon picked herself up and watched the blood trickling down her leg.

'*Oh!*' Sharon moaned. 'It's all Mister Horrible Hardy's fault. Keeping me in for a little thing like that.'

'You wouldn't have thought it a little thing if Amy had called you Fatbum in class,' Julia told her.

'*I* haven't got a fat bum.' Then Sharon looked down at her leg and moaned again. 'Oh, it's real bad. And there's the march on Sunday!'

'What march?' Amy said.

'Church parade, of course. I must be right for that.'

Amy was puzzled. Usually Sharon didn't even bother to turn up for church parades.

'The Townsville Drum Majorettes are coming for Harvest Festival.' Sharon limped into the butcher's.

Mr Bone, his hands red from weighing liver, went quite pale at Sharon's knee. Mrs Bone came from behind the cash desk. '*Whatever have you done?*'

'Fell over, didn't I?' Sharon scowled.

'A fine drum majorette you'd make,' her mother said sharply.

'Oh Mum,' Sharon wailed. 'If I was one I'd never fall over again.'

'I haven't got time to take you all the way to Townsville. Neither has Betsy. And there's not the money for it either.'

'It's not fair!' Sharon wailed.

At tea-time Mrs East said, 'Do you know what that traffic warden called the Sunny Stores' price cuts? *An Act of God!*'

Mr East raised his floury eyebrows. 'Albert Pounce thinks he *is* God.'

Mr East frowned. 'Now then, Fred.'

'Well, he certainly thinks he has a hot line.'

Brian picked up a pretend telephone and held it to his ear. 'Hallo there, God. It's me, Albert. I've booked ten people for parking today. Good, eh? Oh, and God . . . These High Street people are getting themselves in a proper tizz because the Sunny Stores are after their customers again. See to it, will you?'

'Look what you've done, Fred East.' Mrs East leaned over the table and clipped Brian's ear. 'Turned your son into a *heathen*.'

Baby Roy shot his milk all over the table.

'There's another one,' Mrs East said.

Amy decided to keep a close eye on Mr Pounce next Sunday in church. Her father had been joking, but . . . just suppose Mr Pounce *did* have a hot line? A thing like that could come in useful.

After tea Brian turned on the telly, and there was Amy's burger. She was pleased to see it again.

As Mr East sat down a shower of flour fell off him. 'One thing I do know,' he said gloomily. 'We can't afford to let our sales drop any lower. Things are looking real bad.'

'Oh Fred,' Mrs East whispered. Instead of clearing away the tea things she sat on the sofa and picked up the jumper she was knitting Amy for the winter.

Brian and Amy looked at the telly, but they weren't really watching.

'I can help,' Brian said.

'Doing what?' His mother knitted furiously.

'Sorting at Pepper's.'

Mr East shook his head. 'I doubt it, son. When things get tight there'll be no sorting.'

At Sunday breakfast Brian said, 'You were right, Dad. There's no more sorting at Pepper's. But . . . Amy and me, we've been talking things over.'

Amy nodded. They had, last night. At least Brian had talked, and she'd listened, until she'd fallen asleep.

'We've decided,' Brian looked very serious in his Cubs uniform, 'we can make do without spending money. And we don't want any Christmas presents this year either. In fact, we'll be very angry if we get any. Won't we, Amy?'

Amy nodded, but her fingers were crossed beneath the skirt of her Brownies uniform.

'Of course Baby Roy will have to have just one or two,' Brian went on.

'And why is that, son?' Mr East asked.

'Because . . . well, he's new.'

'He won't know the difference then, will he?'

'No, but we shall,' Brian said. 'And if we had Christmas presents when we were babies it's only fair he should too.'

Mrs East stopped knitting. She went and put her hands on Mr East's shoulders. '*All* my children will have Christmas presents, or I'll know the reason why.'

'We know the reason,' Brian said.

Fruity came out from under the table wagging his tail.

'If we could find *him* a good home it would help.' Mrs East set about the table.

As the Brownies marched up the High Street, Amy thought it had been the worst breakfast ever. She wanted to tell Julia about it, but the Boys Brigade Band and a whistling wind made it impossible.

One of the drum majorettes in front dropped her drumstick, slowing them down. A pot full of orange autumn flowers blew into the gutter, and Archie darted out from the head of the Cubs to stand it safely inside Pepper's.

The church looked really beautiful inside. Flowers everywhere, and food of all sorts in front of the altar. Red apples, yellow pears, purple plums, carrots and cauliflowers from Pepper's. A big bread sheaf with a rope plait round. Mr East had a special baking tin which came out of his cupboard ever year.

Bone's had sent their usual ham. Everybody knew it was made of plastic, but they also knew that several real ones would be sent to the poorest people in Steeple Foley. As would the rest of the produce.

There was nothing from the Sunny Stores.

The Brownies sat in pews behind the drum majorettes. Sharon gobbled them up with her eyes. Amy watched, then looked away and . . . there was Mr Pounce!

The first hymn began.

'*We plough the fields, and scatter the good seed on the land. . .*' Mr Pounce had his eyes closed, but his mouth wasn't making the right shapes for the words. He must be on the hot line!

Halfway through the second verse Mr Pounce opened his eyes. He was singing the proper words again! Now I can get on the hot line, thought Amy. She shut *her* eyes . . .

Nothing happened at first. It was very dark. Then Amy felt sort of peaceful and the dark grew lighter. She began to say, moving her lips but very quietly, '*Please God. I hope you can hear me and you're not getting too many calls through at once. Can you do something to make us earn enough money. It doesn't matter, honestly, about Christmas presents, but if Fruity had to go . . .*'

Julia nudged her.

Amy opened her eyes, but by the time she had found where the hymn had got to it had finished. She looked all round the church. Everyone's eyes were wide open. The hot line was shut down.

There were more hymns later, but Amy didn't risk a second try.

At the end of the service Mr Pounce came round with the collecting plate. As Amy put in the money her mother had given her she looked up and . . .

Mr Pounce had a burger floating above his head!

'*AMY!*'

Julia was shaking her arm, and she was surprised to find they were outside the church.

'You've been acting peculiar all morning!'

134

As they walked down the High Street Amy told Julia about the burger.

She waited for Julia to say she'd gone barmy. But Julia nodded. 'That time I thought you'd stopped being my friend a polar bear came out of the bathroom and chased me downstairs. Sometimes it got into the school playground, and followed me home. Then after we were friends again it went away.'

Amy felt relieved. But she kept the hot line to herself.

That afternoon when Fruity had his bath

Brian and Amy took turns hugging him dry.

After they'd climbed into their bunks Brian said, 'If Fruity goes I shall run away.' Amy pretended she'd fallen asleep and hadn't heard, but she lay awake for ages.

A few days later another Sunny Stores leaflet went the rounds of Steeple Foley.

When Amy came home from school Mr East was glaring at it. ' "*Ladies in Love! Crumbly shortbread hearts filled with yummy jam. Dreamt up by our very own pastry cook!*" Not content with taking my customers they've pinched my jammy hearts an' all!' Flour puffed off him in spurts.

'Oh, Fred!' Mrs East clasped Amy to her apron.

Brian came bursting in. 'Archie's gone.'

'Gone where?' Mrs East asked.

'To fix up the van.'

'Nothing but trouble.'

Brian shook his head. 'The van's not broken down. Archie's fitting it out with shelves and things. While Red's dad runs the shop Archie is going on the road.'

Mr East still looked grim.

'Archie says it's no use waiting to be clobbered. Archie says we got to fight back. *Do* something . . .'

'We could sell burgers,' Amy said.

Everybody was looking at her. Mum, Dad, Brian, Baby Roy in his pram. Even Fruity had poked his nose through the curtain.

Brian found his voice first. 'That's something the Sunny Stores don't have, a burger bar.'

Mrs East shook her head. 'There's no room for another counter.' But Mr East was pointing to the opposite corner. 'Do away with the wedding cake that's been with us from the day we opened?'

'You won't get rid of a silly old thing like that,' Brian said fiercely. 'But you'd boot out Fruity.'

A bus pulled up and the shop went dark.

Mrs East smoothed her apron. 'All I said was, *if* he could be found a good home . . .'

But the children had gone. Brian and Amy, carrying Baby Roy, went upstairs to give Fruity a huge amount of hugging. Then they took him out for a huge walk all round the park.

Next day after school the bakery looked different. Amy was just trying to decide why when . . .

CRACK!

Mr Pounce was rubbing his head and scowling. 'What's happened to the old faithful?' He nodded at the corner.

The wedding cake had gone!

'Nothing in this town stays the same for five minutes,' the traffic warden grumbled.

'The fact is,' said Mrs East, 'We're setting up a snack bar. Selling burgers, sandwiches, and filled rolls.' She smoothed her apron. 'We have to do something, Mr Pounce.'

The bar started up on a sunny autumn Monday. Amy and Julia raced out of school to find Mrs Stranger at the gates.

'It's going well,' she told them. 'Piles of sandwiches went off to the Midland Bank. And the burgers were very popular. You should have smelt the library. Mrs Read was going round with an air-freshener.'

As Amy passed Pepper's Archie drew up in his van. Betsy jumped off the Townsville bus and came running to meet him.

'Move that van from my yellow line!' a voice roared.

'Just going. Keep your hair on!' Betsy waved at the traffic warden, climbed into the van and away they went.

'Archie says the van is doing fine,' Brian said at tea-time. He looked at his father. 'Archie says he could deliver bread an' all . . . .'

'Now hold on.' Mr East raise his floury, oily eyebrows. 'What Archie says and what I can manage are two different things.' But all the same he looked pleased and thoughtful.

So did Amy and Brian. Things were perking up. They rested their feet on Fruity's back underneath the table.

'*Burgerwurger*!' Baby Roy had cut two more teeth, and his hair was growing. He was beginning to look quite handsome.

It was dark every night now before Amy and Brian climbed into their bunks.

'Brian,' said Amy. 'Mr Hardy gave me a star today.' But Brian had a new torch battery and was reading. 'Remember the hot line? Well, I got on it, and that's how the burger bar started.'

'Mm.'

'Brian?'

'Mm.'

'You've got a face like a fried egg.'

'Mm,' said Brian.

Amy thought of all the things that had happened in the High Street since Harvest Festival church parade.

Archie delivering. Mrs Bone's new Christmas club. Ivor Pollock's fantastic front. The Pig and Whistle was flying a Union Jack, and Jersey Joe had big notices plastered on his windows. *SUPPORT OUR LITTLE HIGH STREET SHOPS. YOU NEED THEM AND THEY NEED YOU.*

As Amy's eyes closed she said silently, 'Thank you, God.'

10
Amy Goes to London

The success of the burger bar meant new rules at the bakery.

Breakfast was at seven o'clock. Mrs East made sandwiches and rolls, while Mr East prepared the burgers. Amy and Brian helped before they went to school. The shop opened at half past eight.

The weather turned.

'It's bad enough keeping the shop clean with all the extra customers,' Mrs East grumbled. 'I can't have mud upstairs an' all.'

So when Amy and Brian came home from school they took off their shoes and left them at the foot of the stairs. One day there was a whole pile—Amy's, Brian's, Red's and Julia's—and

Mr East tripped over them.

He had a big bruise on his forehead. Then a burger spat at him and burnt his nose. And his hair began to turn grey.

Mrs East was most upset. She went to the living-room mirror and found two grey hairs of her own.

'I don't know what you're worrying about,' Brian said. 'All old people have grey hair.'

Mrs East smoothed her apron. 'I'll have you know I'm only thirty-three.'

'Only?' said Brian.

Mr East blew up in a cloud of oily flour. Brian was sent to bed without his supper. His father followed him into the bedroom. 'And I'll not have you ruining your eyesight neither.' He took Brian's torch. 'There'll be no more reading in bed.'

Amy had to listen to Brian moaning. After he'd finished with his father he started on Red's. They'd been turfed out of their hiding place underneath the front.

To cheer Brian up Amy crept downstairs and sneaked him a bag of broken biscuits.

Baby Roy was on the move. Crawling

everywhere. Mr East had fixed up two small doors. One at the top of the stairs, the other at the bottom. The big pram had given way to a pushchair.

As soon as he woke Baby Roy pulled himself up and walked round inside his cot.

'Just look at him,' Amy said admiringly.

Brian turned the other way and looked at Andy Tearovski instead.

'But Brian . . . aren't you proud of him?'

'*Proud?* Know what he'll be doing next? Climbing my ladder and getting at my pictures.'

Amy looked at the place where her own picture of St. Paul's had been. Until Baby Roy had crawled over Amy's bunk and pulled it down. It was too crumpled to put up again.

'Look at him now!' Brian said. Baby Roy had hold of Fruity's tail, and was pulling him backwards.

Amy went and lifted her baby brother out. 'One year old next week. And isn't it lucky? It'll be half-term.'

'*Lucky?*' said Brian. 'All you'll be doing is playing nursemaid.'

That was certainly the way the holiday began, until . . .

Mrs Stranger lost one of her contact lenses. It fell out of her eye into the garden and was never seen again. Julia told the tale, all in a rush, after racing up the High Street and pushing her way through the customers in the bakery.

She leaned against the gate at the bottom of the stairs.

'Mummy's going to London to have a new contact lens fitted on Wednesday. I'm going with her. We're staying the night at Jonny's. *And you're invited too.*'

Amy couldn't believe it. She rushed to ask her mother.

Betsy Bone was in the bakery buying buns. 'Stay the night in London? You lucky thing.'

'Oh Mum,' said Amy. 'Can I?'

Mrs East looked over the counter at Baby Roy who'd crawled round to play with Betsy's shoelaces, 'I really need you here.'

'I'll look after this one for you.' Betsy hoisted Baby Roy high in the air. Then she whispered in his ear and he clasped her round the neck. 'Look, he loves me, the little pet.'

'But what about helping Archie on the van?' Mrs East said.

'He doesn't run Wednesdays.'

Mrs East said she'd see.

'There's her fare,' she told Mr East at tea-time.

'Mrs Stranger offered to pay it,' Amy said.

Mrs East shook her head. 'I'll not have my family taking charity. If you go . . . .' She paused to smooth her apron. 'I only said *if*, mind, then we're the ones who'll pay your fare.'

Mr East, all floury and oily, nodded. 'We're doing better trade now.' He patted his wife on the arm. 'Invitations to stay in London don't grow on trees, my dear.'

'You're right, Fred. As long as . . . .'

'*What, Mum?*'

'You don't go getting fancy ideas . . . .'

'*Oh, Mum!*'

'The ones she's had up to now don't seem to have done us much harm,' Mr East said.

Then Mrs East began worrying whether Amy's clothes would be good enough for London. She stayed up late finishing off the winter jumper, and next day they went down to Jersey Joe's and bought an almost new tartan skirt. A freshly-washed anorak, shining shoes, clean socks, nightie, toothbrush and comb made up the rest.

'Don't forget to polish up your brains as well,' said Brian.

It wasn't until everything was laid out ready on her bunk that Amy realised a terrible thing. Wednesday was Baby Roy's birthday.

'I can't go,' she told Julia.

'Yes you can. You'll be here in the morning to say Happy Birthday.'

But Amy had to be ready by six to catch the early train. It was still dark, and Baby Roy was fast asleep.

'Happy birthday,' she whispered, putting the toy drum she'd bought at Jersey Joe's into the cot.

Mr East looked round the door. 'Come along, Amy.' Mrs Stranger's car was outside to drive them to Townsville station.

Jonny Wopping lived in a flat in London, but it was very different from the one over the bakery. They went up in a lift, then along a corridor to a front door with a big brass letterbox. The rooms inside seemed enormous. And everywhere there were books.

At first Amy thought Mr and Mrs Wopping were Jonny's grandparents. They both had grey hair. Jonny wandered in with his nose in a book.

Julia nudged Amy. 'He's Mister Nobody again.'

'No I'm not,' Jonny said. 'Two pages to go and then I shall be at your disposal, ladies.'

Julia and Amy went to the bathroom to have a giggle. They sat on the edge of the bath and Amy nearly fell in. It was the biggest bath she'd ever seen, and over the top on a shelf were . . . *more books!*

Jonny came and found them. 'Julia said you'd like to see St. Paul's,' he told Amy.

'You mean . . . *real St. Paul's?*'

Mr Wopping took them. He got up from his computer, and waved to Mrs Wopping sitting at another computer. Mrs Wopping waved back, and went on tapping.

'Uncle James writes books on science,' Julia explained as they followed him to the lift.

147

'Auntie Polly writes cookery books.' And all they'd had for dinner had been soup and bread and cheese!

Amy had never been on the Underground before, and she loved it all. The sliding doors on the trains. Escalators in the stations. And all the different sorts of people.

They came out to the sky again and . . . there it was. St. Paul's Cathedral. Exactly like her picture.

To Amy's surprise it was crowded inside. 'People come from all over the world,' Mr Wopping said. And I've come from Steeple Foley, Amy thought proudly. She looked up into the vast Dome.

'That's my favourite place.' Jonny pointed. 'The Whispering Gallery.' Amy saw people, like distant dolls, walking round inside it.

They climbed so many stairs Amy lost count. When they reached the Whispering Gallery Jonny made her stand with one ear to the wall. Then he walked away from her, and went on walking.

'What's he going to do?' Amy asked.

'Wait and see,' Julia told her. 'And listen too.'

148

At last Jonny stopped. He waved, and leaned against the wall. 'Amy,' came a voice in her ear. 'Can you hear me?'

'Yes I can!'

'Don't shout. Whisper.'

'Yes I can,' Amy whispered.

'That's better.' Jonny was right across the other side!

'The Dome was built to catch and carry sound waves,' Mr Wopping explained. Then a whole lot of people came up, and the wall began humming like a telephone exchange.

They climbed up above the Dome and looked out over the great city of London.

'I'll never forget this,' Amy said.

When they returned to the flat it smelt just like the bakery.

Mrs Wopping was in the kitchen surrounded by bottles, pots, packets, pans, books . . . Amy saw *Cakes and Pastries of the World*. And then she remembered Baby Roy's birthday.

Julia looked at her. 'What's the matter?'

Amy whispered in Julia's ear. Julia went and told her mother, and Amy was led to the telephone.

'Amy!' Mrs East didn't sound over a hundred miles away. 'What's happened?'

'Nothing, Mum. I've just rung to see if Baby Roy enjoyed his birthday.'

'Well, Dad baked a special little cake, just like that drum you gave him. Yes, the drum was a great success with Baby Roy. I don't know about the rest of us. He had quite a party. Red, Archie, Betsy and her sister . . . .'

'*Sharon*?'

'Yes. I hope you're being a good girl?'

'I'm just going to have my tea.'

'I'd better ring off then, or we'll run up a bill. Tell Mrs Stranger I'll pay for the call. Goodbye, Amy.'

'Goodbye, Mum.'

'What did she say?' Julia asked.

Amy told her.

'Did Baby Roy blow out his candle?'

'I don't know.'

Tea at the Woppings wasn't tea, but dinner split into lots of bits. Amy hardly tasted it. All she could think of was Sharon taking *her* place at Baby Roy's first birthday.

'Aren't you enjoying your dinner, Amy?'

Mrs Stranger asked.

'Oh yes.' Amy made sure she ate everything, whatever it was.

Last came little chocolate éclairs. Amy noticed *them* because they were exactly the same as the ones in *Cakes and Pastries of the World*. To her horror a pair of tears rolled down her cheeks, making puddles on her plate.

'I know,' Mr Wopping said. 'Let's have a treasure hunt.'

While the grown-ups made up the clues and planted them about the flat the children were locked in the bathroom! Outside so much giggling and rushing about went on that Amy cheered up and forgot about being homesick.

The first clue was easy.

Dry us in the sun,
Watch us wrinkle.
Cook us in water,
We'll be smooth
In a twinkle.

'Prunes!' they all said together.

Julia found them in a glass jar on the kitchen shelf. The next clue was tucked underneath.

After that the clues became more difficult

151

and harder to find. They were in all sorts of places. Underneath carpets. Inside cupboards. Down behind the furniture. One was stuck on the sole of Mr Wopping's shoe. And the last but one was inside the grandfather clock.

As Amy reached for it the clock struck . . . half past ten! How could it have got so late?

'Haven't you found that treasure yet?' Mr Wopping called.

'Nearly,' Jonny said.

'Well, hurry up,' his father told him. 'It's high time you were all in bed.'

They took the clue away to the kitchen.

'If I know Father,' Jonny said, 'the last clue will be a stinker.'

'Let's have something to eat then.' Julia began looking in the tins. They collected quite a feast, and this time Amy tasted it all.

Then they got to work on the clue.

My name is CAPOTW.
When you have found me
Open the golden gates.
Inside is your treasure!

Nobody knew what CAPOTW meant.

'Knowing Father it's a code,' Jonny said.

But they couldn't crack it.

'Perhaps it's Polish, or Greek or something,' Julia said.

'What about the golden gates?' Amy asked.

They went everywhere and searched every-thing that looked in the least like a gate. In and out of all the rooms, fetching up at last in the box room where Amy and Julia were to sleep.

Amy climbed over a couple of suitcases and sat on the bed.

'She's going broody again,' Jonny told Julia.

'No she isn't. She's thinking.'

They were both wrong. Amy was trying to keep awake. She'd never been up so late in her life! At home everyone would have been asleep long ago. In a few hours' time Mr East would start the morning baking!

BAKING?

Amy opened her eyes wide. 'I know what those letters stand for!' She leapt over the suitcases, rushed along the corridor to the kitchen and took down . . . *Cakes and Pastries of the World.*

Jonny cheered. '*Well done*! Now all we need are the golden gates,'

'Waffles,' said Amy.

Taped inside the page with the waffles were three packages, and inside them three golden pound coins. The grandfather clock struck again.

Midnight!

The next day the children didn't wake until halfway through the morning. After breakfast they said goodbye to the Woppings. On the way to the station they went to Selfridges and spent their treasure. Amy bought a golden bauble.

At least, that's what Mr East called it when he saw it.

Mrs East frowned. 'Where did you get this?'

'I bought it from Selfridges.' Amy told them all about the treasure hunt. Mr East smiled when he learned where the treasure was found, and who had found it.

'Whatever next?' Mrs East smoothed her apron. Amy decided not to tell about staying up until midnight.

Baby Roy wanted the bauble but Amy whisked it out of reach. 'That's not a birthday present. It's to hang on the Christmas tree.' He yelled and yelled because he couldn't have it.

'He's spoilt with all those people making a fuss of him,' Brian said. 'Thank goodness you're back. Don't you ever let Sharon Bone come here again.'

'It wasn't my fault,' Amy said. 'What did she do?'

'First she wouldn't eat anything else but cakes. Then she pinched the best ones. She kicked Red under the table. Red kicked her back, but got Archie instead. Archie sent him home. Then Betsy got upset and made Archie fetch Red back again. Sharon wouldn't leave Baby Roy alone. *She* was the one who blew out his candle.'

At bedtime Brian was reading on the sofa.

'Aren't you coming to bed?' Amy asked.

'No, I'm not ,' Brian replied. 'There's been a new rule since you've been away. *I'm* allowed to stay up half an hour later. Goodnight.'

11
Amy and the Dummy Christmas Pudding

Christmas was coming. Out came the decorations, and Amy and Brian helped Mr East make a Christmas window. Turkeys hung waiting in rows in Bone's.

The day school broke up the children were allowed to take toys of their own. Sharon brought a drum.

'It's as bad as being at home,' Amy told Julia. 'I made a terrible mistake giving Baby Roy that drum. Brian's hidden it away in Dad's store cupboard.'

Mr Hardy overheard.

'What a good idea, Amy.' He put Sharon's drum in the cupboard, and Sharon with it!

At playtime she marched round the

playground drumming. Once she threw both drumsticks in the air, *and caught them!* Which made her more puffed up than ever.

It was Julia's turn for tea with Amy. As they reached the bakery a bus drew up and Betsy stepped off. She followed them inside.

As soon as Baby Roy heard her voice he came crawling round the counter.

'How's my pet then?' Betsy hoisted him high in the air. Amy couldn't help feeling a bit jealous. 'I'll take ten buns, and ten of your jammy hearts, Mrs East. Sharon's having friends to tea.'

'She hasn't invited anyone from school,' Amy said as she carried Baby Roy upstairs.

'And she didn't *say* anything,' Julia added. 'That's even more peculiar.'

Baby Roy pulled himself upright and bashed on the sofa.

'At least he hasn't got the *you know what*,' Julia said. 'Does he know it's in the store cupboard?'

Amy shook her head. 'He's forgotten all about it.'

A bus drew up outside. When it had gone

there was a lot of noise. Amy and Julia ran into the front bedroom and opened the window.

Down below was a crowd of girls, getting in everybody's way.

Mr Pounce came hurrying along. 'Now then. I can't have you cluttering up my pavement.'

'Who are they?' Julia asked. 'They seem familiar, and yet . . . .'

Then Amy recognised the girl who dropped her drumstick at Harvest Festival. 'They're Townsville Drum Majorettes. And they're going into Bone's!'

Amy and Julia went back to the living room . . .

'*BABY ROY!*'

Fruity was hiding under the table.

'I'm going to fetch Mum.' Amy made for the door at the top of the stairs, climbed over and went down two at a time to the bottom.

'*MUM!*'

Mrs East frowned. 'What have you done?'

'It's not us. It's Baby Roy. He's *walking*!'

Mrs East left Amy to look after the shop while she went up to see for herself. Amy sold a rye loaf and a Russian cake to Mrs Read. Six sausage rolls to a hungry-looking cashier from the Midland Bank. And the last Christmas pudding to Charlie Dickens, the bookseller.

Then Mrs East called downstairs.

'*Fred? FRED!*'

After Amy had sold out on buns and jammy hearts Mr and Mrs East bowled through the curtain. They were smiling and smiling. Mr East looked like a pink and white zebra. His smile lines were full up with flour.

'Your brother's not a baby any more, Amy. From now on he's plain Roy.'

'Yes, Dad.'

Brian and Red came bursting in.

'Bone's is full of girls,' said Brian. 'There's a hundred at least.'

'Now then, don't exaggerate.' Mrs East smoothed her apron. 'There are certainly no more than ten.'

'Ten girls are like a hundred normal people.'

'Never mind girls,' said Mr East. 'Go upstairs and see what a certain small *boy* is doing.'

The Saturday before Christmas there was a procession through Steeple Foley. Amy took

Roy upstairs to watch from the window.

'*DUM, DUM!*' He beat on the window when he saw the Boys Brigade drummers, followed by Father Christmas on a giant sleigh. And there was Sharon, a full-blown drum majorette now, her nose triumphantly in the air, until . . .

A potato dropped off Pepper's front and rolled in front of Sharon's feet. She kicked it. The potato rose in the air, just missing Father Christmas.

'Snowing spuds now, is it?' he said in a wobbly voice.

When they'd gone Amy carried Roy downstairs. 'I know who Father Christmas was,' she told her mother, 'Jersey Joe.'

Mrs East frowned and nodded at Roy.

'He doesn't care. All he wanted was to see the drums. Oh, no. I've done it now!'

And she had!

'*DUMDUMDUMDUMDUM!*' roared Roy until . . .

CRACK!

Mr Pounce stood rubbing his head. 'A Christmas pudding, if you please.'

'We've sold out,' Mrs East told him. 'But

Fred is making a fresh supply. I'll put one by.'

'Fresh?' Mr Pounce was horrified. 'Christmas puddings need to mature, like wine.'

Mrs East smoothed her apron. 'You should have ordered one sooner, Mr Pounce. I thought perhaps you'd buy one at the Sunny Stores.'

'Do I look like a man who buys cut-price Christmas puddings, madam?' The traffic warden strode to the door.

'Be careful,' Mrs East warned, but . . .

CRACK!

Amy was sent to the kitchen to remind her father about the extra Christmas puddings.

Mr East hadn't forgotten. But there were other things to prepare. Chocolate logs. Mince pies. And Roy was on the loose looking for *you know what*.

'It's on the shelf next to my little pudding basins,' Mr East told Amy. 'Hold on to Roy while I open up.'

But Roy's eyesight was sharp as a crow's. The moment the cupboard was open . . .

'*DUM! DUM! DUM! DUM! DUM!*' He wouldn't stop.

Mr East lost his temper, whisked the drum

from the cupboard and put it outside in the yard. A cold wind blew in. Roy collapsed in a floury heap, sat on the floor and yelled and yelled.

Amy flew upstairs, two at a time, with Fruity flying in front of her. Fruity shot under the table and stayed there, while Amy grabbed the dummy.

'It's all right, Mum,' she told her mother as she passed the curtain. 'I'm fixing him.'

Roy hadn't sucked his dummy for ages. He was quite pleased to see it again, and let Amy wipe his damp little face. 'Yuck, you're like an uncooked pie.' There was even a currant in his hair.

Brian and Red came into the kitchen.

'Did you see the new drum major . . .?'

'Stop,' Amy warned. But it was too late.

'*DUMDUMDUMDUMDUMDUMDUM!*'
Roy drummed with his fists. He drummed with his heels. He made more noise than the whole of the Boys Brigade Band playing together.

'Enough is enough.' Mr East pointed a floury finger. 'Take that little monster away, out of my kitchen.'

The dummy had vanished. As Brian and Red carted Roy upstairs Amy searched, but she couldn't find it. Neither could Brian or Red when *they* searched.

Red fancied himself a detective.

'Imagine,' he said, when they'd all returned upstairs. 'You have a fabulous jewel and you want to keep it safe.'

'Put it in the bank,' said Brian.

'Don't be barmy. I'm talking about *his*'— Red nodded at Roy— '*you know what.*'

'You said a jewel.'

'I was just giving an example.'

'What example?'

Red groaned. 'Think of the scene of the crime then.'

'What crime?'

'Listen. Do you want to find the *you know what* or don't you?'

They all looked at Roy. His eyes were half-closed and he was sucking his thumb.

'We're bound to need it again before Christmas gets here,' Amy said.

'Answer this question then.' Red pointed at Amy. 'Exactly where was the criminal when you last saw the *you know what*?'

'If you mean Roy, he was by the big mixer.'

'And was the *you know what* in his mouth?'

'Yes. No. Wait a minute . . .' Amy remembered. He was holding it.'

'So the criminal removed the *you know what* from his mouth. And then?'

'I'm not sure,' Amy said. 'Wait a minute. Yes I am. He threw it!'

'Aha!' The detective was very pleased with himself. 'And it didn't land on the floor or the table because we checked. So . . .'

'It went in the Christmas pudding mixture!' said Brian.

They rushed downstairs but it was too late. All the little puddings were cooking in their basins.

'Back again?' Mr East said.

They crept upstairs.

'I've heard of money in Christmas puds, but never a baby's dummy,' Red said.

'Perhaps it will melt away,' Brian said hopefully. 'And nobody will ever know.'

'But Mum puts it in boiling water to sterilise it,'Amy said. 'It doesn't melt then.'

Red nodded. 'She's right. The dummy will come out much the same as it went in.'

They turned to confront the criminal, but he'd gone to sleep.

'We've got to get it back,' Brian said. 'If somebody found *that* inside their Christmas pudding . . .'

'You'd probably be closed down,' Red told him. Brian told Amy it was all her fault for fetching the dummy in the first place.

Betsy called up the stairs. Archie wanted Red and Brian to help unload some Christmas trees.

Amy put Roy safely in his cot, and went down to serve in the shop. The customers came in looking as though they'd been sprinkled with icing sugar.

Snow began to settle, making the bakery window look more inviting than ever. The smell of Christmas pudding and mince pies spread through the shop and out into the High Street. Customers lingered.

Closing time came.

'At last!' Mrs East told Amy to turn the notice from OPEN to CLOSED. '*Just look at my floor!*'

Brian trailed another lot of snow across. Then Mr East asked whether anyone had thought to take Fruity out. Nobody had.

So Amy and Brian put on their outdoor shoes and coats to walk Fruity down the High Street.

The Sunny Stores were open late. There were notices plastered across their windows. CUT-PRICE CHRISTMAS PUDDINGS WITH A SURPRISE INSIDE!

'If they knew what our surprise was!' Brian said.

Next morning the children listened for Mr East to come for his breakfast. Then they raced downstairs.

On the kitchen table sat the Christmas puddings in greaseproof paper with their tops open.

'Couldn't be better.' Brian picked up two skewers and gave one to Amy. 'You start that end. I'll start this.'

Sticking the skewers into each pudding they covered the holes as they went. They were just about to meet in the middle when . . .

'Leave those puddings alone!' Mr East stood in the doorway. 'Your mother wants to get breakfast cleared.'

Amy almost told, but Brian tugged her away.

They ate their breakfast as fast as they could.

'What manners!' Mrs East smoothed her apron. 'Pigs at a trough could be better!'

And when they'd helped to clear away and run down to the kitchen again . . .

'You can help me shift these pudd'ns,' said their father.

Amy and Brian looked at each other helplessly. The puddings were all *in their wrappers*.

Much later, after Fruity had had his bath and been rubbed dry in front of Mr East's bread oven, Amy said, 'If only we'd told!'

'It's too late now,' Brian decided.

Mrs Stranger bought the first two puddings. Mr Stranger would be home, and the Woppings were coming to visit.

'Polly Wopping, the famous cookery writer, eating my Fred's Christmas pudding on Christmas Day!' Mrs East couldn't stop smoothing her apron.

All Mr East would say was, 'If only she'd bought one of my early ones.'

'If only,' Brian said to Amy, 'she hasn't bought the one with the dummy!'

The day before Christmas Eve Amy went to tea with Julia. They stuck skewers into Mrs Stranger's puddings, but there was nothing inside but fruit and nuts.

By Christmas Eve there were five puddings left to be sold. The bakery wouldn't open again for three days, and there was a queue right down the High Street.

Loaves and loaves of bread were bought.

Brian helped his father carry trays from the kitchen to the shop. Mrs East and Amy served. Mince pies, sausage rolls, cheese straws, croissants, jammy hearts, chocolate logs, Christmas cakes, Christmas puddings . . . .

All the world came in.

Mrs Read. Miss Wright. Charlie Dickens and Ivor Pollock. Mr Hardy. Jersey Joe. Betsy Bone. Jessie Owen and her mother. Mr Pounce. Great-Gran Pepper . . . .

'Happy Christmas, one and all.' She cackled like a cheerful parrot.

'Are you sure you should be out in the cold?' Mrs East asked.

'Never felt better in my life, dearie.'

The queue moved forward.

CRACK!

Great-Gran turned and poked Mr Pounce in the ribs. 'Somebody should give you a crash helmet for Christmas!'

'I don't receive Christmas presents, madam.' There was a shocked silence. 'All I allow myself is one Christmas pudding, to remind me of my family.'

'It's hard being alone at Christmas, dearie.'

Great-Gran ordered some extra mince pies and handed them to Mr Pounce.

Mrs Owen bought him a bag of cheese straws. Betsy Bone invited him for Christmas dinner, but Mr Pounce thanked her and said he'd prefer to stay quietly at home. Then he wished everyone a Happy Christmas and walked to the door.

'Careful,' Mrs East called. And for once Mr Pounce remembered.

After a while the queue disappeared and the customers faded away. While Amy strapped Roy in his pushchair Brian fastened on Fruity's lead. They went out into the High Street.

Most of the shops were shut now. Bone's was bare and empty without its turkeys. From the Pig and Whistle came the sound of Christmas carols. Red came running out from Pepper's with four oranges, one for each of them. Under the mistletoe Archie was kissing Betsy.

The dummy was never seen or heard of again. Someone must have bought it because all the puddings were sold. But after Christmas Mr Pounce brought Roy a present. It was a little plastic crash helmet.

HIPPO BOOKS FOR YOUNGER READERS

If you've enjoyed this book, you'll probably be
interested to know that there are loads more Hippo
books to suit all kinds of tastes. You'll find scary spooky
books, gripping adventure stories, funny books, and lots
lots more.

Alex and Roy: Best Friends	
by Mary Dickinson	£1.75
The Little Gymnast by Sheila Haigh	£1.25
Something Lost, Something Found	
by Val James	£1.50
The Broomstick Academy by Robin Klein	£1.25
Nellie and the Dragon: Whatever Next?	
by Elizabeth Lindsay	£1.75
The Ghosts of Hungryhouse Lane	
by Sam McBratney	£1.95
Beware, this House is Haunted!	
by Lance Salway	£1.95
The Little Vampire	
by Angela Sommer-Bodenberg	£1.25
Harriet and the Robot by Martin Waddell	£1.50
The Practical Princess by Jay Williams	£1.50
Perkins by Linda Yeatman	£1.50

You'll find these and many more fun Hippo books at
your local bookshop, or you can order them direct. Just
send off to *Customer Services, Hippo Books, Westfield
Road, Southam, Leamington Spa, Warwickshire CV33
OJH*, not forgetting to enclose a cheque or postal order
for the price of the book(s) plus 30p per book for postage
and packing.

STREAMERS

We've got lots of great books for younger readers in Hippo's STREAMERS series:

The Little Yellow Taxi and His Friends

| | Ruth Ainsworth | £1.75 |

Sally Ann At The Ballet   Terrance Dicks £1.75
Sally Ann – The Picnic £1.75
Sally Ann Goes To Hospital £1.75
Sally Ann – On Her Own £1.75
Sally Ann – The School Play £1.75
Broomstick Services   Ann Jungman £1.75
Tom   Ruth Silvestre £1.75
Nate The Great   Marjorie Weinman Sharmat £1.75
Nate The Great and The Missing Key £1.75
Paws: A Panda Full Of Surprises
    Joan Stimson £1.75
Aristotle Sludge   Margaret Leroy £1.75
The Old Woman Who Lived In A Roundabout
    Ruth Silvestre £1.75

You'll find these and many more fun Hippo books at your local bookseller, or you can order them direct. Just send off to Customer Services, Hippo Books, Westfield Road, Southam, Leamington Spa, Warwickshire CV33 0JH, not forgetting to enclose a cheque or postal order for the price of the book(s) plus 30p per book for postage and packing.

JUGGLERS

There are books to suit everyone in Hippo's JUGGLERS series:

Pet Minders	Robina Beckles Willson	£1.75
The Jiggery Pokery Cup	Angela Bull	£1.75
The Ghosts of Batwing Castle	Terry Deary	£1.75
Stan's Galactic Bug	John Emlyn Edwards	£1.75
My Friend Robinson	Anne Forsyth	£1.75
As If By Magic	Jo Furminger	£1.75
Bags Of Trouble	Michael Harrison	£1.75
The Spooks	Elizabeth Lindsay	£1.75
The Secret Of Bone Island	Sam McBratney	£1.75
School Trip To The Stars		£1.75
Horrible Henry and The Headless Ghost		
	Kara May	£1.75
When I Lived Down Cuckoo Lane	Jean Wills	£1.75

You'll find these and many more fun Hippo books at your local bookseller, or you can order them direct. Just send off to Customer Services, Hippo Books, Westfield Road, Southam, Leamington Spa, Warwickshire CV33 0JH, not forgetting to enclose a cheque or postal order for the price of the book(s) plus 30p per book for postage and packing.